MY ΣX FRΩM HELL

TELLULAH DARLING

TE DA MEDIA / VANCOUVER

Published by Te Da Media, 2013

Library and Archives Canada Cataloguing in Publication

Darling, Tellulah, 1970-
    My ex from hell / Tellulah Darling.

(The Blooming goddess trilogy ; bk. 1)
Issued also in electronic formats.
ISBN 978-0-9880540-3-5

    I. Title. II. Series: Darling, Tellulah, 1970- Blooming goddess trilogy ; bk 1.

PS8607.A74M9 2013   jC813'.6   C2012-906914-0

Front Cover Design: www.ebooklaunch.com

When the going gets desperate, the desperate send email

To: ????
From: bloomingoddess@gmail.com
Subject: Seriously?

Dear Your Royal Imperialness Demeter, Goddess of Grain and Fertility, Preserver of Marriage, and Bringer of Seasons,

Or can I just call you Mom?

Bet you never thought you'd be hearing from me. Sorry for not having written sooner, but until about twelve hours ago, I didn't know you existed. Nothing personal.

See, yesterday, I was plain old Sophie Bloom. My life sucked in your typical 16-year-old ways. I was stuck here at Hope Park Progressive School on probation *again* ("mouthy behavior"), dealing with cliquish poseurs, rampant hormones, blah blah blah.

Then I met a guy. I know that's the worst cliché ever. But sadly, it's true. And of course, me being me, he couldn't be just any bad boy. No. He had to be Kai, son of Hades, Lord of the Underworld. Anyway, he was really hot and there was this bone-melting kiss and … whatever. The point is, before he showed up, I thought I was human. Afterward, well, let's just say everything changed. Who knew when I was cramming Greek mythology for my English final, I was studying the family tree?

They say when you die, your whole life supposedly

flashes before your eyes. When Kai and I kissed, here's what flashed before mine—Mount Olympus, Zeus, the Underworld, Hades, and you. But that wasn't my life. Or was it?

Here's the Wiki version. (Do you have Wi-Fi on Mt. Olympus?) Turns out I'm Persephone. Me, Goddess of Spring and Embodiment of Earth's Fertility? Ew! Which makes me your kid, Hades' target, and totally screwed. In the myth version, I'm the innocent maiden, you're the grieving mother, and we're reunited with great joy. Guess that's why they call it a myth.

I know I sound like a nut bar. And maybe I'll wake up in a padded room restrained for my own safety. But in that moment with Kai, it felt *real*. Like I knew who I was. Or used to be. Those were *my* memories flashing before my eyes—not some fantasy or hallucination. Part of me remembered those moments. But where do I go from here? And is there an online tutorial I can take?

I don't exactly have your email. But if you're a goddess, maybe you'll know I'm writing. That I really need my mom right now. And if not—well, I guess I'll save this for my obituary. Which I'll probably need pretty soon because of the gods-wanting-me-dead thing.

Take care.
Sophie

a.k.a. Persephone
a.k.a. Goddess of Spring
a.k.a. Your Daughter

1
All's fair in high school and war
α′

Let me state, on the record, that despite that super melodramatic email, I am totally sane. Well, as sane as I can be for a sixteen-year-old. I've just had the day from Hell. Literally.

I should back up. Hi. I'm Sophie Amalia Bloom. Longtime human, first time goddess. How would I describe myself? Hmmm. If my life was going to be a movie—do you ever do that? Rescript your personal history with a great soundtrack and better extras? My dream version would be courtesy of Tim Burton but I think the sad truth is that the movie of my life would be a lame after-school special.

You know, something like "poor little rich girl, her life littered with hopes and dreams." I love "littered with;" such over-the-top drunk divorcée lingo, uttered right before the aging cougar smashes her cocktail into the fireplace. Just how my adoptive, socialite mother Felicia ended every New Year's Eve. But we have plenty of time to get into moms and their respective failings.

My life in a nutshell on Saturday, October 31, when my universe turned upside down, involved me being a totally human junior at Hope Park; a "progressive" day and boarding school whose forward-thinking curriculum was offset by the students' petty jealousies, social climbing, and the ongoing dramas of hook-ups and break-ups.

The only bright spot was that it was Halloween. Sure, it meant a dance with far too many dumb boys in drag (acting out some of their not-so-latent sexual issues), but it also meant chocolate.

And dressing up.

And revenge.

Cue horror music and the entrance of the dreaded yoga girls. The leader of that "namaste" bowing bitch-fest was one Bethany Russo-Hill. For all her practice of enlightenment through bendiness, she ran her ~~cult~~ yoga sessions like a drill sergeant. Girls had been known to come out sobbing because their sun salutation wasn't worshipful enough.

To say I hated that red-haired, black-souled cow would be an understatement. My greatest fantasy was to poison Bethany slowly, then let her get better before administering a really nasty dose that left her dead and rigor mortised in a humiliating position. Emphasis on the humiliation. The dead would be a happy bonus.

Since she had been at Hope Park as long as I had, Bethany and I had a nice long run together. It wasn't any one big torment, just a continual series of small cruelties. But as Bethany was Miss School Spirit, managing to fool the Powers That Be with her big blue eyes and Googled new age crap, I was the one currently on probation due to my attitude problem.

But thanks to some laxatives, a wig, and one unforgettable kiss, the balance of power was about to shift.

See, for the past twenty-four hours, Bethany had been going on and on about some town boy she'd met on a field trip. Apparently he was so hot, she'd set up a drunken midnight rendezvous with him.

I caught this dirt as I was coming out of the principal's office having been lectured once again on the importance of cooperation and getting along with one's classmates. Oh, and I had earned that probation status I mentioned, due to an earlier encounter with Bethany that was just now screwing me over.

Bethany had seen me chewing on the end of my pencil and spread the rumor that I liked to "suck wood." Charming. So I went up to her and told her that she might like some tips since the only way she'd ever get ahead in this world was on the basis of her oral dexterity. Guess which one of us was overheard.

All this to say, I'd had enough of her Bindi-wearing rule of tyranny. As Bethany seemed so excited about her little tryst, I could think of no better plan (well, not on such short notice anyway) than to wreck it for her.

Laxatives ground into the bottle of vodka she planned to get hammered on before the dance: ten dollars. Bribe money for Stan the janitor to go out and buy me a wig in town that exactly matched Bethany's dark red hair: twenty dollars. The joy of impersonating Bethany and making her out to be a giant twat? Priceless.

The plan was to sabotage her hook up with a poo party. Not only would she miss the midnight meeting, but if I was lucky, she'd experience loud, gaseous humiliation. Meanwhile, dressed in my Bethany yoga costume (which would irritate the hell out of her), *I* would go find the guy at the meeting spot by the back fence and make such a fool of my Bethany persona that he'd never want to see *her* again. Brilliant, right?

The first up in the naysayer parade was my best friend, Hannah Nygard. If Hollywood ever drove a money truck up to my door and begged to make the aforementioned movie of my life, Hannah wouldn't even need beefed up stunt casting, thanks to her genetically superior Swedish good looks. Yes, of the tall, blonde, leggy, chesty variety. She even has perfect posture.

'Course, when I met Hannah, we were both six and she was covered in dirt and letting black ants run over her arms. She's a big science geek. Had I known that she'd become this bright, glorious sun and I'd be the space junk trailing in her wake, I might have had second thoughts about sharing my Creamsicle with her on that first day. But maybe not.

Me, on the other hand? I'd need an A-list actress to replace my low-rent, cable-show-passable normalcy. Average height, average brown hair, below average chest. As for my wardrobe: I went for funky comfort over flaunt my booty. Honestly, what would be the point? I'd still be more "kinder" than "whore." Leggings stuffed into flat boots with short skirts and layered shirts suited me fine.

Apparently, though, there was still hope for me. I had this on good authority from my adoptive mother Felicia, who turned to me last summer and pronounced: "I've seen a lot of uggos, kid. And you're not going to be one of them. There's a pretty good chance you'll grow into your looks." Textbook positive parenting. I would have run to Daddy for an ego boost, but since that position had been filled by a revolving door of stepfathers, it was kind of a no go.

Felicia would never have said that about Hannah. The two of us were as different as best friends could be. Fabugeek and the average kid. And fabugeek was currently oozing anxiety. To a casual observer, it would just look like Hannah was scarfing M&Ms. But I knew her. And her scarfing was done with an attitude of extreme worry.

I studiously ignored her as I placed a couple of bowel blowout tablets between two pieces of paper towel on my worn, wooden desk.

"I'm not sure this is a good idea ..." she began, sprawled across her bed on her side of the room, dressed in her standard jeans and geeky science T-shirt. Today's read "Darwin is my homie-nid."

Breezily, I cut her off. "Sure, it is. With any luck, by this time tomorrow, Bethany will be gone."

Hannah gasped. "Sophie!"

I rolled my eyes. "Not dead, dummy." Although a girl could dream. "Just gone. Expelled for drunk and disodorly."

Hannah didn't even snicker at my pun. "I don't know. What if something goes wrong with the dosage? What if she dehydrates?" Hannah was the biggest softy ever. Unlike me and my running character assassination monologue, she found the good in everyone. Usually worried about them, too. Unless there was the off chance of somebody being mauled by a shark, dismembered by lions, or ravaged by fire ants. Then it was all food chains and nature's balance. Girlfriend's love of wildlife wandered into extreme bloodlust territory.

I turned puppy dog eyes on her and put on my most pathetic voice. "Don't you want her bullying to stop?"

She folded her arms crossly, opened her mouth to speak and—

"You know that only makes your boobs look bigger, right?"

Hannah hurriedly uncrossed her arms. She curled into a dejected little ball, even crinkling her candy packaging in a pathetic way.

I felt awful. "I'm sorry. I'm sorry. I'm sorry."

Hannah rose with a grin, sticking her tongue out at me. "Ha! You're so gullible."

I really was. Muttering something about "with friends like these," I raised the boot in my hand to bring down upon the unsuspecting pills.

"No!"

"Seriously?"

Hannah shook her head at me in exasperation. "Not 'no, don't.' No, don't use your boot. You'll just grind the pill dust into the treads. Use my Exacto knife."

I obediently retrieved the knife, which was easy to find due to its place on Hannah's side of the room. It was pretty obvious who slept on which side. Hannah's half was meticulous, with reference books, telescope, microscope, and field hockey equipment all in its place. My side wasn't so much messy as haphazard. It was filled with random stuff I'd deemed cool or important over the years; a Tamagotchi (long dead due to excessive beatings and candy feedings), the bouquet Hannah and Theo had given me for my sixteenth birthday, now dried, the Dr. Seuss book "Fox In Socks," of which I had a dim but happy memory of being read to by Felicia. Stuff like that.

The entire room was raspberry, since once you hit high school, students were allowed to choose their own paint colors for their walls. A girly delight. Or a dark berry nightmare, depending on the light. Over the years, both Hannah and I had threatened to paint the entire thing white but laziness won out. Raspberry it was.

Hannah continued with her directions as I hesitated over the pills with the knife. "Don't smash down. Chop. In fine motions. Also, did you calculate for milligrams versus liquid, taking body weight in as a factor?"

"Huh?" I was lost.

"Did you figure out exactly how many pills need to go into the amount of booze Bethany will be drinking, taking her weight into account so you just give her the runs. Instead of, say, death by defecation?"

"Uh, yes?"

She held out her hand imperiously. "Give me the pills."

I handed them over. "Size of bottle?" she asked.

"Mickey," I replied without hesitation. "About twelve ounces."

"How are you so sure?"

"I bribed Stan an extra ten to tell me what he'd gone into town to get her."

"Okay. She's about a hundred twenty so …" She did a few mental calculations. "Two more please."

I tossed them over to her. "I so love you for your brains."

She sighed wearily. "That's what they all say. But in the end, it's my beauty they clamor for." She handed me back the pills. I placed them on top of one sheet of paper towel and took up the knife.

"Trust me," I said, "unless I start playing for a very different team, I'll never clamor for you."

"You could, you know."

I paused my chopping to throw her a weird look. She glowered at me. "Not me, obviously, because that would feel like incest—"

"Wow. Just keep sticking that foot in deeper."

Hannah rolled her eyes in exasperation. "What I mean is that it would be okay if you liked girls."

I put down the knife and checked the pills. Perfectly ground. "Mom, are you trying to say you'd love me even if I was Lebanese?"

"I wouldn't love you because you annoy the crap out of me, but I would be very happy for you. As long as she's a good person and treats you right."

"Hannah, you're seriously freaking me out now. Did I miss some episode of 'A very roommate moment?'"

"It's just that you never seem to get crushes on guys."

"I don't get crushes on girls, either."

"I know. I was kinda hoping you did and just didn't want to tell me about it."

"One, I wouldn't be ashamed if I did. And B, why were you hoping?"

Hannah impatiently pushed her hair off her forehead. "Because you're sixteen and you should like someone. It's not normal."

That kind of rocked me. I mean, I knew most of the school thought I was weird. If they thought of me at all. But Hannah? "You think I'm a freak?" I asked carefully.

"Only sexually. Maybe physically. Definitely mentally."

I snatched her candy away. "Bite me. Besides, who do you like? Other than possibly gay, pretty boy actors, whose pictures you like to rub up against when you think I'm asleep?"

"I so do not."

"You rustle."

"You're confusing that with the sound of your waterproof sheets. For your bedwetting problem." She threw me her best "don't mess with my superior intellect" expression. "Besides, a gay crush means never making a fashion faux pas. Also, getting great home decorating advice for free."

"Basically, you want an eye candy cliché," I said.

"An eye candy cliché who I'll have a crush on. Which, as I was saying, is normal."

I snorted my laughter. "I bow before your logic." I tossed some candy into my mouth and relented at Hannah's pout to throw a few over to her. "Have you ever considered that being stuck at Hope Park just doesn't give me many chances to meet someone who isn't a total knob? Maybe once I get out of here, I'll meet some guy and it'll be fireworks. He'll be my soulmate. The one I can't live without."

Hannah rolled over onto her stomach. "Jeez, Soph. Drama queen much? I'm just talking about liking some guy. No fireworks. Just chemistry and mutual interests and compatibility."

"You should totally write Valentine's Day cards. 'To my chemically compatible partner. Hope we enjoy a mutual interest together on this fine day.'"

She pulled her pillow, decorated with pictures of sharks, from under her belly. "Then on the back I could include the email for dad's divorce firm. Get a commission for each referral."

"Now you're thinking. I'm off to find vodka." I left the room to her protest of "leave the candy." Which I didn't. But hey. There's friendship and then there's peanuty bites of cocoa delight.

There I was, sugar blissing down the hallway and absolutely not thinking that my words about my fated soulmate were going to come back and bite me in the ass in about seven hours.

To be fair, it wasn't a long bliss out either, since the dorms at Hope Park were set in the short part of the school's L-shaped structure. Our gender-segregated bedrooms and bathrooms were separated by connecting doors on each floor that were supposed to be locked.

Hope Park may have billed itself as forward-thinking but when it came to co-habitation, it was strictly Victorian.

The school itself was a rambling three-story, red brick building nestled in Vancouver Island's Cowichan Valley, off the west coast of British Columbia. The long part of the main building greeted visitors as they came up the winding driveway. It housed the office, classrooms, gym, and cafeteria. The building was pretty airy, lots of windows—all the better to see students practically wipe out on their butts on the totally-worn-and-slippery-but-we-call-them-charming wood floors.

Felicia dumped me in this slice of rural heaven back in grade one. Most definitely as a boarder. So while I was on a first name basis with some of the cows that roamed outside school property, I couldn't always say the same about her husbands. Which was probably for the best. Why bother getting to know expendable Number Six when he was only going to be dumped for being too sporty, not sporty enough, or whatever reason Uncle Oliver cited in the divorce papers? Oliver being Felicia's lawyer and Hannah's dad.

I checked my watch. Bethany and her crew would still be at yoga, downward dogging away, so I knew I had some time to carry out my evil plan. Carefully I slid her door open.

No one bothered to lock up their rooms. For one thing, cell phones were banned (the easiest item with possible dirt on a person) and for another, most of us had the same kinds of stuff. Most of us also had roommates and really, it was very hard to keep a secret in this place.

One way or another, someone was always going to bust you. The closet kleptos were out of luck.

Bethany's room, a rare single occupancy, was a boudoir explosion. One of the wealthiest students at Hope Park, she could afford pricey lingerie and a plethora of cosmetics and designer yoga wear. It was shocking how much companies could charge for clothes made from panda food. Bethany's desire to lord this over anyone who gave a rat's ass extended to the state of her room. I was convinced she never put anything away just so unsuspecting visitors would be forced into up close and personal encounters with all of her privilege. Personally, I found it obnoxious.

Once inside, I stepped over some scarlet Victoria's Secret push-up number and went directly to the giant teddy bear propped up in the corner. I lifted it up, turning the fugly thing over to reveal the jury-rigged bunghole that Bethany had created to stash her booze. It was all very bootlegger. With a shiver of distaste, I shoved my hand into the wrinkly fold.

Success. I pulled the bottle out of its butt. This felt so wrong on so many levels. I unscrewed the mickey of vodka, carefully opened my packet of laxative powder and—

"Sophie Amalia Bloom, you are in so much trouble!" a voice boomed. I jumped a mile, spilling some of my precious stash in the process, and turned with dread to find Theo leaning against the doorframe, busting a gut laughing.

Theo Rockman was the lone male who rounded out

Hannah's and my band of misfits. He didn't enter the picture until grade two so he was a late addition to the pack and, therefore, the most expendable. A fact we liked to remind him of when he got too mouthy.

Theo had spiky black hair to match his thick-framed black glasses and was the kind of guy who wore his wallet on a chain attached to his belt loops. He was the rumpled poster child for charming "nerd-chic." Or a living anime character. He was a little touchy about that comparison though, so I only used it for maximum annoyance.

Theo's parents had died. At least, I think they had. It was never discussed. Except this one time when he was drunk. I assumed (and yes, insert "ass", "u", "me" here) that his mom was some hippy chick because he kept calling her an earth goddess. All I pictured were hairy legs, sensible footwear, and baking bread. I wouldn't have talked about her either.

"You rat bastard ..." I began, desperately trying to scoop up all the spilled powder. "Do something useful and hold this." I shoved the mickey at him.

He glanced at the bottle in surprise as he pushed his glasses back up his nose. "Vodka? Thought she'd be more of a peach cooler girl." He launched into his "commercial voice." "Parents, do your daughters come home smelling like an orchard? Is their giggle quotient higher than usual? They may be in thrall to the dangerous wine cooler. Gateway drug of the terminally insecure, its usage results in excessive clumsiness and the condition 'trophy wife-itis.' The lethalness of which only manifests after age thirty-five and ends in gutter living and suicide."

By this point, I was trying not to pee, I was laughing so hard. "Shut up," I hissed.

He shot me an innocent smile. I added the remainder of the laxative powder to the alcohol. Theo screwed the cap back on and I motioned for him to give it a good shake.

"Neither sleet, nor snow, nor fear of expulsion can keep our heroine from carrying out her incredibly stupid plan," he said.

"Well, you're aiding and abetting now, Einstein. So just stuff good time Charley there back up Teddy and Operation Screw Bethany will be in full swing."

We put everything back in its place and exited the room without being caught. "You really think this is a bad idea?" I asked.

"No. Gastric blowout goes great with probation. Unless you want to stay under the radar and not get kicked out."

"Yeah. Too late for limboing under Big Brother. The pills are dissolving as we speak." I wrinkled my nose. "Nothing is going to go wrong."

"Except the part that has 'complete mess' written all over it."

"Which part?"

"Pick one." Theo flinched as I punched his shoulder. "You figure out how to jimmy the bathroom lock yet, Sophie Magoo?" he asked, using his nickname for me.

"I could use a bit more tutoring."

"Come on, then. If you're determined to do this, better get you in and out as fast as possible."

I linked arms with him. "Thanks, Theo. I appreciate you sharing your criminal skills."

"Don't say I never did anything for you."

Off we went. I felt great. I had a plan and it seemed as if this time, Dame Fortune was going to smile upon me.

Substitute "laugh" for smile, and you'd have been closer.

2
Beauty is in the lie of the beholder
β′

Amidst the hordes of slutty cats, Lady Gaga imper-
sonators, drag queens, and superheroes, Theo, Hannah
and I were definitely "three of these things are not like
the others."

You know how little kids make chains of paper loops
to string on Christmas trees? Imagine two long loops, one
blue, one green, intertwined and strung over Hannah in
her flesh colored shirt and leggings. Yep, my friend had
gone as DNA. Or, as she corrected, "a double helix."

"Did you give yourself an extra chromosome for the
boob gene?" I asked, peering at a loop from our sidelines
of the dance floor in the gym. Shout-out to the decorating committee, they'd really outdone themselves with
that lone disco ball spinning lamely on the ceiling.

"Be nice, or I'll take my hockey socks back." Hannah
started to stuff her hand into my highly padded chest.

I swatted it away. "You made me lopsided." I dug my
hand in and adjusted.

"Dang Soph, show a little class," winced Theo.

I pinned him with my scowl. "Class. Really. Coming
from a guy dressed as a crime scene."

Theo glanced down at himself. "What?"

Hannah and I exchanged looks. Not only was Theo wrapped in a bloody shower curtain, which was held in place by bright yellow "Do Not Cross" tape, he also had a plastic knife sticking out of his liver. I often thought that Theo was morbid beyond his years.

Once I fixed my chest, I was quite happy with my costume. My bamboo yoga wear was hues of mud and sand, supposedly very Gaia chic. They were left over from the one time Felicia dressed me up and sent me out to the yuckapalooza that is hot yoga. My long, red rayon wig was masterfully cut in the same layered locks as Bethany's. A red Bindi sat squarely between my eyebrows and I'd even henna tattooed my hands. I was a vision of "white chick oms out," which, considering who I was impersonating, was perfect.

Anil Patel, star wrestler and main meathead at our school, strutted up to us and posed in front of Hannah. His attempt to make his muscles as large as possible was at odds with the crack whore dress and smeared red lips he sported. Not to mention his hot accessories of cauliflower ears and taped-up fingers. This season's must-haves for the fresh-from-the-mats young wrestler.

Two kinds of kids attended Hope Park: the rich ones, whose parents stuffed them here so they could get on with running huge corporations, arms dealing, or just pretending they're still young and fancy free, and the others, put here for ideological reasons. Their parents liked the fact that we sat around in discussion groups instead of rows, that we were (in theory) supposed to be responsible for our own learning, and that no subject was taboo to explore. All in all, it was a pretty diverse student body.

Seeing how Hope Park attracted the wide range of kids that it did, you think that we'd all be outcasts on some level. One giant "Breakfast Club." Alas, no. I don't know if it was biological imperative or conspiracy theory, but somehow it was always the jocks and the cheerleaders who were the popular kids. My school might not have believed in sports like basketball or football meaning no cheerleaders, but we had the equivalent. Hope Park's philosophy of "celebrating the individual" just meant our popular kids were wrestlers, track stars, and, of course, Bethany's crew.

The guys tended to leave me and my friends alone, probably because they were hoping to get into Hannah's pants at some point and figured that jamming her friends' heads down the porcelain throne would be a real deal-breaker.

Didn't mean I couldn't give them maximum grief.

"I'm guessing that's a costume and not you finally announcing your lack of a dick to the world," I said to Anil.

"Nice trying to go as an actual chick, Bloom," he sneered back. "Maybe one day you won't need the socks."

In the improved movie version of my life, I came back with the best comeback ev-ah. Then inflicted him with fiery butt pain. But there in the gym, I am horrified to say that, yes, I glanced down to see if I was showing, causing Anil to guffaw. He'd got me. I did require sports socks for my chest.

If looks could kill, I'd have blasted his fat head into satisfying smithereens. As it was, the DNA stepped in to protect me.

"Back off, asshole, or you might find a Lonomia caterpillar in your bed," Hannah threatened.

Anil lifted his hands up in mock terror. "Ooh. Wouldn't want it to cocoon me to death."

"No worries on that front." Hannah got that dreamy look that told me she was about to describe an animal kill.

"Uh-oh," Theo muttered.

"This fuzzy baby would flatten your kidneys, then make your red blood cells explode so you hemorrhaged internally. If you're lucky, you'd die."

"Like you have one. *If* it even exists," Anil retorted.

I had to give him points for keeping up his bravado.

Hannah leaned in toward him and tilted his chin up with one finger. "I can get anything online, Sugar. Want to test me?"

Anil swallowed, uncomfortable.

"So leave Sophie alone," Hannah demanded, punctuating the order with a poke to his shoulder that made her chest shake and Anil stare in dumb silence.

That most excellent threat had just died by boob jiggle-age.

"Drool much?" a mocking voice broke in.

I whirled to find Bethany behind me, in a bejeweled

sari that must have cost more than entire Indian villages lived off in a year.

She glanced at my costume with disgust. "Wannabe."

"So says Miss Exotic Other. How many children were harmed in your cultural appropriation?"

"It was a purchase to aid a women's collective in Rajasthan."

I made a gagging motion at her Indian accented pronunciation.

"So much hostility," she soothed. "I know a great pose for relieving stress. It involves shoving your head up your ass."

"I couldn't steal your signature move. Oh wait. That's shoving your head up the teachers' asses. My bad."

Bethany opened her mouth to say something but instead gave a loud fart.

"Gross," Anil summed up.

I contained my utter glee that my evil plan was working and instead fanned the air in front of my face vigorously.

"It's my high fiber diet. At least *I* won't drop dead at thirty," she retorted and flounced onto the dance floor.

Anil turned to Hannah. "Wanna come enjoy a private party that'll blow your mind?" Yup. Her rack had definitely wiped all potential danger signals from his hypothalamus. (Living with Hannah for years had taught me a thing or two.)

She slitted her grey eyes in disgust. "I'd rather have spiders lay eggs in my brain."

"A date with Anil would run a close second," Theo commented dryly.

Anil didn't find that funny. Away he stomped.

Hannah immediately shrugged the encounter off. "Oooh. I love this song." She grinned as the opening strains of the Bee Gee's "Stayin' Alive" came on. The portion of the evening catering to the teachers stuck chaperoning us. Turning their crankiness to happiness through nostalgic boogie down.

Hannah enthusiastically began to sing along, getting all the words wrong as usual. "To the right. Do me, 'kay. You make love the other way," she mangled before stopping dead at Theo's burst of laughter.

"Those aren't the lyrics, you idiot," he snickered. "'Other way?' What did you think? Someone had an extra penis? Or used a foot or something?"

Hannah went bright red. "Doggie style. As opposed to missionary position. Makes perfect sense." Her lame attempt at a logical explanation only made Theo laugh harder.

"Death by caterpillar is still on the table, Rockman," she growled.

I put my arms around their shoulders. "Friends, don't fight. This is a happy night. Now keep Bethany in view so we can enjoy her gastric discomfort. I need to get to the bathroom before she does."

I was counting on her using the staff bathroom over the girls' one off the gym. The one whose lock I'd had Theo teach me how to jimmy. It was private and conveniently located by the exit that led to the back field.

In the event that someone caught me, I'd just say I was worried Bethany was going to make a horrible mistake by meeting this strange guy, and while my strategy was perhaps misguided (locking her in the bathroom), it was all for her safety. Desperate times and all that. Basically, lie my way out of trouble.

After the number of talks we girls had gotten from the school about stranger danger, I had to be believed.

I pulled Theo and Hannah out onto the floor with me. The next little while, I hung out and had a good time dancing with my friends. Sabotaging Bethany was the farthest thing from my mind. Until 11:30. That was when I noticed Bethany making freaky twitching faces. I excused myself to grab some water. A cool refreshing drink, then it was time to put stage two of the plan into motion.

You're probably thinking that my plan didn't work. Well, ha ha, it totally did. Perfectly.

Boy, do I wish it hadn't.

Ten minutes before midnight, I was lurking in the shadows of the hallway by the open bathroom door.

"Are we hiding or seeking?" a voice asked from close behind me.

I jumped, thwacking my ankle in the process. "Jeez," I muttered, shaking it out. "Put on some cat bells, Cassie."

Cassandra Jones. A bit of a loner. A bit weird. But nice enough. She was dressed in wild colors befitting her gypsy costume, her ginger curls bobbing around her pixieish face. Usually, I would have chatted with her, but not tonight. I didn't want anything wrecking my plan.

"Just taking a break from the fun," I replied, all casual.

"Ah." She stood there, head tilted to one side, looking at me. Then she gave a little shiver. "Bethany's coming."

Yup. I could hear her around the corner, chatting to her main suck-up, Veronica Chen. Veronica modeled herself after Bethany in looks and attitude, her only individuality being the high, sleek ponytail she always wore. I could just imagine the rapt expression on her face as she listened to her idol.

Cassie placed a hand on my shoulder. "Watch yourself," she cautioned. "All kinds of things can happen at midnight on Hallow's eve." Then she slipped off down the hallway.

I stared after her for a second, concerned, before shaking it off. There was no way she could have known what I was about to do. Just Cassie being Cassie.

I slipped behind the open bathroom door and pressed my back against the wall.

Bethany was still with Veronica. I held my breath. I couldn't pull this off if Veronica hung around.

"If I need you to wipe my ass, I'll hand you the toilet paper. Now back the hell off." Bethany was such a charmer. I heard Veronica stammer her apologies and flee.

Bethany was now running as she rounded the corner into my hallway.

The click of her heels grew louder and louder. I held my breath, keeping to the shadows as much as possible.

Bethany whipped into the bathroom and slammed the door behind her. As she groaned and her bowels let loose, I jammed up the lock as I'd been shown. With any luck, Bethany would think she'd locked herself in. The perfect perpetrator-less crime.

I'd done it. For once, I was going to have the upper hand and make Bethany hurt. Not huge amounts of hurt, since she didn't even know this boy, but it would always bug her—missing out on what could have been the hottest hookup of her life—and that was good enough for me.

I jammed on a cute black hat that I had at the ready. Identical to Bethany's hair from a distance, my wig wasn't up to close scrutiny and with the hat, it would just be the dark red ends sticking out. That ought to fool the guy. I darted through the exit into the moonlight.

It was one of those perfect fall nights. Unseasonably warm with the right hint of chill and autumn crispness. Still, the sight of all the plants giving one last hurrah of color before dying always made me a little sad.

I took a moment to breathe in the clean, country air and marvel at the silvery landscape. The moon was full and fat and seemed to wink cheerfully at me.

The grass was damp beneath my shoes as I bounded out toward the back fence. Our school's entire grounds were surrounded by a fence. Not a large one, more for show. Or so I thought. It was one of those chest-high, chain link deals, easy enough to hoist yourself over. Not that I ever had. I'd never gone out of bounds unless forced to in science class. There was just more grass, then some pine woods, and I didn't see the attraction.

I later realized that my lack of interest had more to do with me than any deficiency on the countryside's part.

After a few moments, I reached the back fence. There was no one around. I couldn't believe it. All that effort I'd gone to and the dumb guy hadn't even shown. Not that I blamed him. He'd probably only promised to meet Bethany as a way to get rid of her. If he'd even existed at all.

I was just about to turn and leave when someone moved out of the shadows. "Hey there, handsome ..." I drawled in what I hoped was a sultry voice. I know "handsome" was beyond lame but as I'd opened my mouth, I'd realized I had no idea what his name was.

He glanced up. The moon was behind him so I couldn't see his face clearly. He seemed to have dark hair and be wearing jeans and a leather jacket but that was about all I got.

"The name is Kai," he corrected.

How to put this without sounding stupid? Aw, screw it. There is no way. His voice made me tingle and shiver and warmed me in places that definitely should not have been warm at that moment. Think of every bad romance cliché and you're getting close. Kai's voice was dark and lazy and slightly foreign and ... whoa baby, I'm getting weak just thinking about it.

Name, voice, it all worked for me. Fortunately, he couldn't see me nod like an idiot puppy at his words.

I'll give Bethany props for this. Based on voice alone, this guy could have been the world's ugliest dog and I'd still get why she made the date with him. Although I was totally hoping the face would do the voice justice.

Kai came slightly closer. Not near enough to reveal

his face, but close enough for me to notice he was taller than me, with broad shoulders. I guessed he was about six feet to my five feet, five inches. Very promising.

"Wasn't sure you were going to come," he said.

I put my Bethany voice back on. "Of course I was, silly." I added 'casual' into my voice repertoire. "Enjoying the moonlight?" Yeah, I was knocking that witty banter out of the park.

Kai continued to move closer, until it was just the fence separating us. The voice inside my head cheered. *That's it, buddy. Come closer and let me see the goods.*

I almost lost my breath. He was that good looking. He was maybe about seventeen, but he'd outgrown that awkward boy-to-man phase. Before me stood a fine male specimen with dark hair that curled slightly at their ends, eyes the color of my favorite strong espresso, and wearing a spicy cologne that I found myself leaning into to inhale like a crack addict.

Suddenly, I didn't want him to think that I was Bethany. What was I supposed to do, though? Pull the wig off and look like some little kid pulling a Halloween prank?

If I went through with my original plan of making him think that Bethany was dead weight, he'd probably bolt to get out of spending time with me. Her. I weighed my options.

Even if I did get Kai to like me as Bethany, the chances of him meeting her again and realizing he'd been duped were slim. Which meant that I could have this night, Bethany would lose out, and then Kai and I would go our separate ways.

I was a veritable mastermind of strategic planning.

He shot me a cocky grin. "You gonna come out and play, sweetheart?"

Insolent puppy. My total crushing on this dude was at odds with my natural inclination when hearing something like that to shoot off some sarcastic comment. I clamped my lips firmly together, swung my leg over the fence (big props for stretchy yoga wear) with only a moment of hesitation, and hopped down on the other side.

"Better?" I raised an eyebrow. Two could play at this cocky thing.

Kai shrugged and pushed a lock of hair out of his eyes. "It's a start." He sat down on some spongy ground and patted the place next to him. "It's dry."

I sat down. Now, I'm going to be brutally honest. I had no idea what to do or expect. While I'd kissed a couple guys before, there'd been build-up. This whole "hello stranger, take me" scenario was unfamiliar territory. Should we talk for a while? Or just cut to the physical part? Exactly how much would that physical part involve? I hadn't really thought this through.

"So. What's your story?" He turned dark eyes my way and it felt like my answer actually mattered to him.

"You know. Mom and Dad from rival families, forbidden affair, love child produced. Parents disappeared, leaving me rich beyond my wildest dreams but alone, and I continue to hope they'll come back so I can know love." I turned big, blinking eyes on him.

This was the period piece version of my life and way

better than the true "adopted by a drunk socialite, stuck at boarding school in middle of nowhere, catch me in ten years when I actually have a life and a story" reality.

He stared at me for a second. A long second. An extremely long second in which I thought that maybe normal people don't give weird melodramatic and fake life stories to total strangers. I'd forgotten that I wasn't with Theo and Hannah and maybe this didn't actually fly in the real world. Two minutes in and I'd already blown it.

Then he laughed. Hard. Relief swamped me.

"I wouldn't have thought you were this funny," he said.

Relief turned to indignation. "Why not?" I bristled, completely forgetting that he was referring to Bethany, not me.

"Chill. Just thought your type would care more about looks than humor."

Now I was indignant on Bethany's behalf, which was a real feat. "My type?" I asked sweetly.

"The kind of hot chick who wants to grow up and land some rich guy." He was right about Bethany in that regard. Still.

"You've had a wide sampling, have you? Gotten to know all us chicks intimately enough to know our hopes and dreams?" I kept a smile on my face but from his flinch, it may have looked more feral than friendly.

He smirked. "Yeah. I've been intimate."

That killed it. Dude was such a douche. "Wow. Well, I'm underwhelmed. And cold now. So I'm going back in. Have a nice life. Hope you don't die naked in a closet after your sugar mama's husband shows up and shoots you. Because we all know your type." I stood up and took a couple of steps back toward the fence.

I jerked to a stop as he grabbed my arm in a really strong grip.

"Sweetheart, you have no idea of my type." There was something ominous in his tone.

Outwardly I remained calm, but inside I was seriously freaking out. Flirty fun died pretty quickly when a strong stranger had you at his mercy.

While Hannah and Theo knew where I had gone by this point, they wouldn't bother coming to find me yet. I was out here alone with some random male who could easily kill me and dump my body in the woods where it wouldn't be found for days. I swore if I ever got out of here, I'd follow the advice of every boring safety talk the school ever gave us.

I desperately didn't want to die before I'd really lived. Maybe I could bluff my way out. I forced myself to make eye contact with him. "Let go," I said evenly.

Thankfully, he did. Kai raised his hands in compliance and took a step back. He stared at me, really stared, as if he was trying to figure something out.

Then he reached out and tugged my wig off. My fab locks of sweaty, wig-smashed hat head fell lankly down. "Nice look."

I knelt down to pick up the hat that had flown off my head and instead found myself lunging for a chest sock making a sudden escape, hoping Kai hadn't seen it.

His sarcastic laugh proved otherwise.

Since I couldn't replace the sock, I pulled the other one out as if it didn't matter. "You're a dick. Let's cut our losses and hope to never see each other again."

"You know, girls don't usually mouth off to me."

"Yeah, yeah. They fall all over themselves trying to impress you." As I almost had. But that was the me of five minutes ago. Way in the past. The current me was all "sisters are doing it for themselves."

He grinned. Almost like he was surprised at my backtalk. "Pretty much. They do."

Before I knew what was happening, he kissed me.

Oh, yes. Oh, deliciousness. And then some. I felt electricity shoot between us. He must have felt something too because he broke it off looking totally dazed. "Who—"

I grabbed him and kissed him again. Small talk later. More kissing now. It was so amazing, I got dizzy and saw lights. Hannah was so wrong about the whole fireworks thing.

My heart was racing. My bones were melting. If Kai hadn't had his arm around me, holding me, I don't think I could have stood. It was like I'd kissed him a million times before, each one better than the last. He was familiar and new and right. And, above all, so *mine*.

A blinding flash of pain nailed my skull. Like someone was ripping my head in two.

I doubled over. Kai caught me and grabbed onto my shoulders to steady me. "Who are you?" he demanded.

"Sophie," I began, as another stab of incredible agony tore through me. But this time it came with visuals. I saw an enormous white and gold hallway, filled with larger-than-life figures.

He shook me. "Talk to me."

I swatted at him.

Flash! Another image. A powerful man was holding court. No, not a man. It was … "Zeus," I whispered.

Kai paled.

Part of me had the presence to acknowledge that I'd look like a ghost, too, if I was stuck with a strange girl having some kind of psychotic episode.

I slumped to the ground, put my head to my knees, and curled up in a little ball, trying desperately to stop the insane images. There was an auburn-haired woman in a flowing robe, whose smile was made of sunshine and who looked at me as if I was the most precious thing in the world. The way a mother would look at her most beloved child.

Vaguely, I was aware of Kai muttering "no, no, no" somewhere beside me. I tuned him out and tried to focus in on this woman. My real mother. I knew it with absolute certainty.

My inner video stream changed. Gone was the place of light. Instead I was in a horrible place. Dark and fiery and full of hate. I whimpered.

My hair was sweaty and plastered to my neck. I was getting colder and starting to shiver.

Kai swore under his breath. Then he bundled me up in his jacket.

I inhaled his scent like a talisman that would keep me grounded.

It did the trick. The pain and the crazy hallucinations went away. I took a deep breath and opened my eyes.

Kai was fixated on me like I was something out of a horror movie. I touched my hair self-consciously. I knew I must have looked like something a zombie wouldn't touch, but Kai could have given me a break. For all I knew, I'd just discovered I had a brain tumor and six months to live.

"Was this all a big game to you?" he demanded.

"More of a joke, but—"

"And I was the punchline?" He kicked the fence, hard.

Time to calm him down and get out of here. "Look Kai, I'm sorry you got caught up in this."

He gave a bitter laugh.

"But the joke was supposed to be on Bethany."

"Stop lying to me."

I jumped at the fury in his voice, shrinking back as I glanced up at him and saw a flat blackness in his eyes. I kept a careful watch on him as I spoke. "I'm not lying! What's wrong?"

"I want the truth. You owe me that much."

This guy was super touchy. Must have had a whopper of a burn from some chick. "Truth: I'm Sophie Bloom. I go to Hope Park. Bethany? She's a giant cow, so I pretended to be her so you wouldn't ever want to see her again. I didn't mean to upset you."

He searched my face carefully. "You're sure of this?"

"Yeah. I wouldn't lie about something that exciting," I commented, my snarkiness plain.

Tension eased from his body. He sat down beside me

and shook his head. "Sorry. For a second I thought … hoped … Doesn't matter. Halloween weirdness."

Cassie's earlier warning echoed in my head and my entire body turned into a giant goose bump.

"Definitely." I agreed, shoving aside all concerns. I turned my head to look at him. "It's been a night to remember. Or not."

Somewhere in the distance, a crow cawed, reminding us both of the lateness of the hour. "I've got curfew so …"

He stood up. "Of course."

I grasped the hand he outstretched and let him pull me to my feet. Then I reluctantly handed him back his jacket.

We stood a moment looking at each other. "Goodbye, Sophie Bloom." He leaned in and gave me the softest peck on the lips.

The boy might have looked scary for a bit but right now, he was so fine. "Goodbye," I said, then clutched my head as the mother of all torment wrenched through it. Along with an image so strong, so right, that I knew it wasn't an image at all. It was a memory.

Of Kai and myself or some version of myself having just made love.

I stared at him, open-mouthed in shock. "Kai?"

His face lit up. "Finally." He kissed me as if his very life depended on it.

This time there were no more painful flashes. No more crazy images. Just bliss.

Until someone ripped us apart, then punched Kai in the jaw and sent him sprawling.

35

3
What doesn't kill you makes you seriously doubt your sanity

γ′

I pivoted around to angrily confront whoever had just wrecked the best moment of my life with a sucker-punch to Kai's pretty face.

"Theo?" I asked, astounded.

His actions smacked of jealousy, but that was so not Theo's M.O. Not over me, anyhow. Theo (to clarify) was gay. In theory. There'd never been a real guy I'd seen him crush on, but the selection available here at Hope Park was hardly stellar. And I figured if he'd been jealous over gorgeous Kai, he would have punched me. So no idea what his deal was.

Other games were at play here and while I seemed to be a participant, I was clueless about the end goal.

I turned to check on Kai. He was gingerly rubbing his jaw but didn't seem to have suffered any major damage. I had to know what was going on. Why did I think I'd had a relationship with Kai before? Why was Theo so mad? How could I get more of those kisses? Suckily, I never got a chance to ask.

"Stay. Away. From. Her." Theo spat out. He grabbed

my hand and with a strength I wouldn't have thought he possessed, forced me back over the fence with him, onto the school grounds.

To be fair (and yes, I was shallow enough to be thrilled by it), Kai tried to get me back. But when he reached the fence, Theo yelled something at him in some language I didn't know he knew and certainly didn't recognize. Whatever he said stopped Kai dead in his tracks.

"This isn't over," he called back to Theo. I caught a final glimpse of him kicking the fence in anger before Theo's sprint forced me to pay attention or risk breaking a leg.

"Ow! Let go, you psycho," I gritted out at him as my ankle bumped painfully over a rock. "You're damaging the goods."

Theo refused to speak to me until he'd shoved me into my room with seconds to spare before bed check. Since juniors and seniors were allowed to stay at the dance until midnight, bed check had been extended from our regular 11pm curfew to 1am.

He pushed me backward onto my bed, with its very excellent thread count. Felicia didn't stint on the linens.

Hannah was staring wide-eyed at the two of us. "Mommy, daddy, please don't fight."

"Stay," he ordered me.

"I'm not a dog," I shot back at him.

"Too bad for me," he muttered and stalked out.

I glanced at Hannah. "Did I miss something at the dance? Who peed in his cornflakes?"

"No idea. One minute we're doing rock paper scissors

to see who'll go get you for bed check and hopefully ruin any fun you're having for being a total monkey butt and ditching us, and the next he storms out. What did you do to him?"

"Nothing."

"You must have done something." She looked at me eagerly. "Let's back up and go into great detail. Did you meet Mr. Stud?"

"Yes." I pulled my pjs out from under my pillow and slipped into them.

"And?"

"I am no longer a crush virgin." I crawled under my comfy blue comforter and lay back against the matching sheets.

"You didn't!" Hannah practically bolted up.

Our guidance counselor Mrs. Rivers poked her head in. "Girls, I know it's been a very exciting night but at least pretend to sleep."

We smiled at her. She was one of our cooler staff. "Sure thing, Mrs. R," I replied.

"Good-night," she said, and shut our door.

The door had barely closed before a heavy Hannah-shaped weight jumped on me. "You total skank. You slept with a stranger."

"Yeah," I shot back. "There I was, out back with some guy I'd just met and I thought 'why not just give it up?' At worst, it'll be bad, fast vanilla sex with only a slight reminder of the night in nine months time. At best it'll be astoundingly slutty."

She cocked an eyebrow. "Which was it?" she asked, sweetly.

"Neither. It didn't happen. I said I lost my *crush* virginity. Emphasis on the crush." I shoved her off me.

She leapt back to her bed and burrowed under her own purple covers. "Did you do anything noteworthy?"

"Kissed." I tried to sound like it was no big deal.

"Reeaaaalllly? Scale of one to ten."

I opened my mouth to say "eleven" and then I remembered all those stupid flashes. Did I have some kind of mental illness? If I subtracted about minus forty for the disturbia factor that left … "It was okay."

Hannah looked at me sharply. "Did something happen? Did he do something to you?"

I wasn't sure how to respond. "Yes, he gave me the world's greatest kiss then triggered an aneurysm," didn't seem appropriate. "Nothing. I think I'm just worn out from all my debauched activity today."

"You'll have to build up your stamina if you're going for that life of crime," Hannah replied. Seconds later, I could hear her deep breathing. Dead to the world.

I wish I could have said the same for me. It was a very long, fear-filled night. Worrying that my brain might explode was actually the least of it. What did those images mean? What was my connection to Kai? There was no way that had been a random meeting. I knew him. On some level. And he knew me too.

Scariest of all was what if I'd just reached my lip lock pinnacle at the tender age of sixteen?

Morning didn't make things any better.

I must have fallen asleep at some point after dawn. I remember light streaking the sky as I stared at my clock, waiting for it to be late enough to call Felicia and ask for a complete run-down on my medical history. Then suddenly, I was bolting upright with a cry of "Bethany!" I dropped my head in my hands. "Brilliant." I'd forgotten all about her.

Hannah applied a light coat of gloss to her lips and rubbed them together before speaking. "You forgot to let her out?"

I squirmed under her gaze. "Maybe."

There was a light knock on the door and Cassie popped her head in. "Are you okay?" she asked anxiously.

Impending brain tumor aside? "Fine. And you?" Poor girl really seemed upset.

"I had a rough night," she muttered, tugging anxiously on the fringes at the bottom of her oversize knit sweater.

Hannah patted her on the shoulder as she headed out with her toothbrush, bathroom bound.

I rooted around in my drawers for what to wear. "You and me both."

Oddly, Cassie perked up at that. "Really? Like, life changing?"

I thought about the images and the entire Kai encounter. "You could say that."

"But you're cool with it?"

If I focused only on the amazing kiss part. "I'd say so."

Cassie enveloped me in a huge hug. "I'm so glad."

I disentangled myself gently. "Me too." Okay, freaky child. Time for you to go.

Cassie threw one more beaming smile at me. "Oh yeah. Principal Doucette sent me to get you."

"No worries, Cass. I won't shoot the messenger."

She grinned at me. "Phew. Wouldn't want you getting all viney on me." She waved her hands around.

I tossed my favorite, super soft red sweater on my bed. "Sorry?"

"You know," she prompted. "The whole Persephone thing."

Who? I must have been staring at her like she was totally nuts because her forehead creased in confusion. "You don't know anything about this?"

"Uh, maybe? Did we study her in English?"

Cassie looked like she might throw up. She grabbed my shoulders and shook me, hard. "You said 'life changing.' You said you were cool with it." She sounded totally panicked.

My surprise at her behavior completely overrode my annoyance at being shaken like a dog with a chew toy. "Cassie, calm down. What happened to you last night?" I put my hand on her arm but she jumped back like she'd been scalded.

"No! Don't touch me!" She bolted from the room, brushing roughly past Hannah.

"What's wrong?" Hannah asked with concern.

"I don't get what just happened. She told me Doucette wanted to see me then freaked out."

"I'll go to her room and check on her," Hannah offered. "You get your butt to the office."

"Here's the thing with Bethany," I started to explain.

Hannah clamped her hands over her ears. "Uh-uh. The less I know, the less they can torture out of me later."

"Hilarious."

Believe me when I say I was so not in the mood to deal with any of this. All I could think about was talking to Felicia to see if there was a family history of Schizophrenia or brain tumors. I had narrowed down my condition to one of the two, just to keep it manageable.

I threw on my favorite outfit, needing fortification through fashion. Black leggings with a fitted short black skirt, topped with the sweater I'd dug out. I pulled my hair back into a ponytail and was good to go.

I was on the verge of walking into the principal's office, declaring my guilt, and getting it all over with if it would get me to a phone faster. But when I walked in and saw Bethany—tear-stained eyes, tissue poised perfectly in hand—being comforted for her "ordeal" (she slept on a floor—big deal), I rebelled.

They wanted the goods on me, they'd have to prove it.

"You wanted to see me, Principal," I asked in my cheeriest voice. It was my attempt at "look at me, I've got nothing to hide."

Principal Doucette straightened. "Sit down, Sophie." Our principal was wearing grey trousers and a button down shirt, same as always. He may have dressed conservatively in his role of educating the fine minds of my generation but his short, neat dreads made me think he was a lot cooler than his professional appearance let on.

He motioned me to a chair. Happily, my favorite one was available. I'd been in that office so many times,

I'd done a Three Bears rundown on the furniture; too hard, too soft, just right. With the large window to my right and a massive bookcase behind Doucette's desk for perusing titles, there were lots of distractions for the inattentive at heart.

I sat down and did a double-take as I noticed a woman sitting off to the side. Maybe thirty, her hair was styled in a short pixie cut and dyed purple. She wore a funky dress with a ton of silver jewelry. Was she Bethany's cool aunt or something?

"Hi, Sophie." She gave me a friendly smile. "I'm Ms. Keeper. Great to meet you."

"It is?" I answered back.

"Ms. Keeper is our new guidance counselor," Principal Doucette explained.

"What? Why?"

He frowned at my bluntness.

I tried to backtrack. "I mean, sorry, but I just saw Mrs. Rivers last night at bed check."

"She had a family emergency she had to take care of," the principal replied. "We were lucky to get a replacement sent in so quickly."

Ms. Keeper grinned at me. "He means I'm low on the district totem pole and work Sundays."

I grinned back. I couldn't help but like her.

Bethany sniffed, loudly, wanting the attention placed firmly back on her. "My chakras are deeply damaged from my trauma."

"Bethany, yes, sorry," the principal soothed. He turned to me. "Do you know why I've called you in?"

So my chakras could be deeply damaged from listening to Bethany? "No."

"A very disturbing thing happened last night. Bethany was locked in the staff bathroom and not found for some time."

It took everything I had not to laugh at her patently fake expression of woe. The internal mantra of "you have a brain tumor and are either going crazy or dying" helped keep me looking suitably sober. "I'm sorry to hear that."

"No, you're not." Bethany turned to Principal Doucette. "She's so consumed with jealousy that she went dressed as me to the dance, then locked me in that bathroom. Buddha says that 'he who envies others does not obtain peace of mind.' She has no peace of mind. Her inner light is diminished. It unbalances her."

Bethany speak for "she's crazy." I couldn't really argue that point so I argued another. "Why?"

"Why what?" she retorted.

"Why did I supposedly lock you in?"

"Because."

"Because isn't an answer, kiddo." All of us turned to look at Ms. Keeper. I was especially shocked to hear someone defend me. Or, if not defend me, then not exactly support Bethany.

I smiled gratefully at Ms. Keeper.

Bethany looked confused. I'm sure she was. She was so used to adults believing her every word that her brain must have been short-circuiting. I hoped her head would explode.

Ms. Keeper looked inquiringly at Bethany. "Well? You must have a reason behind your charge."

I raised an eyebrow and threw a bland smile at Bethany. Even if she could positively identify me, which she couldn't, there was no way for her to nail me without admitting to her planned escapade last night.

Bethany hesitated. "She just doesn't like me." So sad.

"If I didn't like you," I replied, "why did I go as you to the dance? Imitation is the sincerest form of flattery," I pointed out to my new best friend, Ms. Keeper.

She frowned. Whoops. Too far.

"I'm sorry, Bethany," Principal Doucette said, "unless any proof arises, we'll have to assume it was merely a case of a faulty lock."

Bethany lowered her eyes and sighed in a shuddery breath. "May I have extensions on my current projects to restore myself back to optimum energy?"

"Of course," he said.

Miraculously, I manage to keep from gagging. I stood, eager to get out of there.

"One last item, Sophie," he added. "You do admit to dressing as Bethany last night?"

I nodded.

"Did part of that costume involve a red wig?"

"Yes."

"Then do you care to explain how that wig was found outside school grounds this morning?"

Busted.

Bethany brightened.

"I have no idea. I threw it out last night because it was

45

itchy and giving me a headache." The memory of why I'd actually had a headache, complete with every mad image I'd seen, came rushing back to me. I felt nauseous.

Ms. Keeper was concerned. "Do you feel all right?"

I shook my head. "I need to lie down. May I go?"

Principal Doucette glanced at me, probably to check if I was faking it, but whatever he saw convinced him because he nodded.

I stumbled out of his office and into the secretary's area, Bethany on my heels.

She shoved me into the corner of the front office counter, hard, as she moved past me.

That was gonna bruise.

"Sophie?" Ms. Keeper had followed us. "Can I speak with you?"

That didn't sound good. "I was just about to call my mom."

Bethany left, making sure to give our counselor a big smile on her way out.

"One minute. I'm betting you know a lot more about what happened then you're letting on." Ms. Keeper held up her hands to stop my automatic protest of innocence. "If you were behind Bethany's lock-in, then I'm concerned about what might have prompted it. Girls like Bethany are …"

I couldn't wait to see how she finished that sentence.

"Bullies. If that's what's happening, then you need to speak up. I can help you."

Yeah, right. "Thanks. Bethany and I are fine."

Ms. Keeper sighed. "I'm not going to let this go. I

want to help you find your voice. Get empowered. You don't need to live as a victim."

Nice thought. But bullying hardly mattered if I was about to drop dead from a tumor. "Can I call my mom now?"

She gave a reluctant nod. "Of course. If you aren't ready to let me help you, I'm glad you at least have your mom to confide in."

I may have laughed out loud at the idea of confiding in Felicia about anything because Ms. Keeper gave me an odd look. "Yeah. My mom's great," I covered.

She patted my hand. "We'll talk more another time."

The second she left, I booted it to the phone on the far end of the counter, which was specifically for students in the event of an emergency. I figured this qualified.

With shaking fingers, I dialed Felicia's number up at her swanky chalet in the ski resort town of Whistler and prayed that she'd answer.

"Hello?" At least she sounded sober.

I fought back the absurd urge to cry "Mommy, I'm dying." I hadn't called Felicia "mommy" since I was six years old. The desire to do so now must have meant there was something seriously wrong with me.

"Felicia?"

"Sophie? What's wrong? I hope you're not calling for money again. And you certainly better not be in any kind of trouble."

Yup. That killed any comfort fantasies I had about this lady.

Felicia was all about appearances. To have a child be

anything less than exceptional was a huge disappointment. Having a child at all was a huge disappointment, so it was odd she'd adopted me in the first place. I think she'd been trying to impress a guy. Which should give you an idea of the lengths Felicia would go to get what she wanted.

She'd learned to spin the truth about most of my shortcomings—imagined or otherwise—pretty well, but there would be no getting around it if I got myself kicked out. And since my prime directive was to stay on mom's payroll and graduate, buying me time to figure out what I was going to do with my life, I had to suck it up and deal the best I could.

I put on my best "good girl" voice. "I was wondering what you knew about my birth family?"

"God, Sophie. It's far too early for me to remember ancient history like that."

This was going well. "Just the medical history. Any mental illness? Any problems with brain cancer?"

"Don't be ridiculous. You came from a perfectly healthy family. Can you see me taking some sickling?"

She had a point there. "Maybe you weren't told?"

"Sophie, you've barely even ever had a cold. Your robust health is one of the few consistently admirable traits about you." Oh yeah, I glowed at that stunning compliment.

"So don't get all hypochondriac on me now," she admonished.

I had one more question for her. "Am I Greek?"

She snorted in disdain. "Why would I adopt a foreign?"

Which to Felicia meant anyone not of Anglo-Saxon origin, no matter how many generations here in Canada. Oddly, her straightforward racism kind of cheered me up. "This is an exceedingly strange conversation. Are you on drugs?"

"Drugs!" I yelped happily. "That's it."

"What's it?" she asked, annoyed.

"Nothing. Nice talking to you, Felicia."

"Uh-huh. Goodbye, Sophie." She hung up.

I wasn't sick. I wasn't crazy. Somehow I must have touched something or drunk something that had been laced with drugs. Not an impossibility at this school.

Last night, I had sipped from a drinking fountain. That was when it must have happened. Just someone's idea of a Halloween prank. I almost fainted with relief.

I practically skipped out of the office back to my bedroom. I paused at the door that separated the boys' corridor from the girls' corridor in the dorms. The one that was *supposed* to stay locked but most of the time was not, allowing free access during the day between our bedrooms. Now that I was ensured of a long happy life, I wanted to know what Theo's deal was. No time like the present.

After a furtive glance to make sure no teachers were around, I raced down the hallway and threw his door open, revealing his minimalist decor. I knew we'd have privacy because his roommate had been sent home to recover from mono, which he definitely hadn't gotten from kissing.

"What's up with the punching, sunshine?" I asked.

He didn't even look up from fixing the arm on his glasses. "You should be thanking me. You'd have seen six kinds of trouble if you'd been late for bed check. Maybe expulsion."

I sunk onto the brown blanket on his bed. "Then you come out and call me. You don't punch the guy I'm kissing. A little much, don't you think?" I picked up a wind-up fifties style robot from a low shelf, turned the key, and released it on the soft folds of the blanket.

"I did call you. Three times. You were too busy sucking face with Kai to notice."

Whoa. "You know him?!"

Theo shrugged. "We've met."

"Where? Why didn't you mention this?"

He finally looked up. "It was ages ago. I didn't know you were going out to meet *him*. Believe me, if I had, I would have locked you in with Bethany." He took the robot away from me.

"You met this guy, what? On summer vacation?"

"Yeah. We held hands and made out on the beach. Don't be a total muppet. Our families are acquainted."

"Your problem with him is …"

"He's a player."

"I had one kiss with him, Theo. It's not like I was going to be used and abused."

"I didn't want you to get hurt."

Theo's angle seemed plausible, if a little big brother-ish for him. "Thanks for looking out for me, but I can handle myself."

"Not with that dinklord," he said gravely.

I rolled my eyes. "Now who's the drama queen?" I strode to the door, then paused. "What was that language you spoke?"

He glanced up. "Huh?"

"To Kai. Last night. You said something in some language and it seemed to keep him from coming over the fence."

Theo stared at me like I was nuts. "I swore at him. In English. You okay?" He put down his glasses. "Something happen last night?"

"No. Well, maybe. I think someone might have laced the water fountain down by the gym. Because I had all these crazy hallucinations."

Theo looked very concerned. "What kind?"

I couldn't figure out why he looked so intense about this. "Just random, weird trippiness."

He relaxed slightly, gave me a thorough looking over, and turned back to his tiny screwdriver. I guessed that meant I was dismissed.

The entire morning so far had been incredibly strange and draining. Not to mention, I'd missed breakfast. I went back to my room and flopped on my bed. Hannah was peering at some slides under her microscope.

"Everything kosher?" she asked.

"Yup. Cassie?"

"Didn't want to talk about it but seemed calmer."

I frowned. "Did you hear anything about Mrs. Rivers leaving for a family emergency?"

"No."

"She did. We've got a new guidance counselor. Guess

she'll be taking my class tomorrow. Also, I talked to Theo."

Silence. Hannah tended to space out when she was working on her microscope. "Hannah." Still nothing. I crept over, licked my finger, and stuffed it into her ear.

"Brat!" she brushed me off. "What?"

"Five minutes and you can go back to curing cancer. I talked to Theo. He claims the reason he hit Kai while he was kissing me—"

"He hit him? You didn't bother telling me this last night?"

"Keep your panties on." We both snorted at the word "panties" which we agreed to be the most offensive word ever. "I'm telling you now. It's because he's a player. Apparently Theo knows his family."

"Makes sense," Hannah said. "Bethany would pick that type."

"Yeah." I thought a moment. "Zeus had a wife, right? What was her name again?"

"Nice non-sequitur. It was Hera. This is relevant how?"

"Someone laced the water fountain last night."

"Again?"

"Apparently. I had the full ancient Greece technicolor tour of hallucinations, complete with seeing Zeus and Mount Olympus and some woman who I guess must have been Hera."

Hannah finally looked up from her microscope at me. "Was this before or after the kiss?"

"During."

"Seriously?! What if it wasn't the water fountain but his lips that were laced?" she asked.

"Doubt it."

"Stranger things have happened, Neo. And it was Halloween."

"It was, Morpheus. But since I wasn't abducted, thrown into a shipping container, and sent on my way to the Baltics to be sold into sex slavery, highly unlikely."

Hannah gave me a look of ultimate disbelief. "Right. That rack of yours would command such a good price."

"Try my highly prized virginity."

"I dunno. You've done a lot of biking."

I shuddered. "Go back to your slides."

She did. While I easily dismissed her ludicrous theory, part of me still marveled at how nuts the entire night had been. If I had been the one on drugs, why did Kai say "finally" before he kissed me that last time? Unless he was on drugs, too, and we were sharing some kind of bonding moment? Plausible, much? This entire thing bothered me.

I decided to go outside, get some fresh air, and think. There was no conscious plan to end up back at the sight of my tryst. My feet just sort of went there. I leaned on the back fence and looked out.

The area looked normal aside from some freshly over-turned earth. Like a small animal digging something up. Not like Kai burying something.

My stomach contracted in a knot of dread. I was drama queening again. Letting my imagination run riot.

It was a beautiful fall day, birds were singing, and I hadn't fallen victim to a tragic demise the night before.

All was well here. I knew I should go back inside but chose door number two, where I ignored the prickling on the back of my neck to jump over the fence. I scurried toward the site of my alleged near miss.

Leaning forward, I scrabbled at the dirt with my hands like a fiend. I'm not sure what I thought I might find. My cold, decomposing body, proving that everything I'd experienced in the last ten hours was just my soul crossing over?

There was nothing there. I sat back on my heels feeling slightly foolish.

Just as a blast of fire struck the ground where my head had been a second before. Without thinking, I threw myself sideways, narrowly missing being blasted again.

My heart was pounding in my chest, my throat was dry and my brain had shut down except for screaming "Get out!" at me. I was in full-on flight or fight mode. Without the fight. I ran as fast as I could into the woods. The very dense, dark woods.

I was too terrified to even look around at what was attacking me. Desperately hoping it wasn't Kai come to finish what should have happened last night.

Adding a new level of horror was the fact I could smell fire from whatever my tormentor was throwing at me. I was in a forest full of lovely crisp fall leaves and dry pine needles with a madman aiming fireballs at me. The phrase "I was toast" had never seemed so real. Or sinister.

Out of the corner of my eye, I saw a large boulder and

dove behind it, shimmying on my belly farther back to a stand of cypress tress I could hide behind.

Carefully, I poked my head out to see what lunatic was on my trail and got the fright of my life. Jason in a hockey mask wielding a chainsaw would have been a more welcome sight.

Picture if you will the figure from Munch's "The Scream" covered entirely in flames and floating about four feet in the air.

He must have heard something because he whirled around sharply and elongated his arm to impossible lengths to send out a tentacle of fire. It was to my credit that I didn't pee my pants in that moment.

A man-shaped creature landed hard on the ground beside the wraith. Like he'd just dropped out of the heavens. Which made no sense but seemed perfectly rational after the appearance of the incredible combustible dude.

I say "creature" because while he seemed to be a bald wall of muscle similar to any guy found at a biker bar, he was seven feet tall with a tattoo of a gold thunderbolt snaking over his head and freaky, glowing gold eyes. I could see their light from fifty feet away. Throw in a pair of stretchy leotards and a mask and this 'roided out aggressor would have made a fortune on the WWF circuit. Snap his opponents like twigs.

Infernorator, the fire floater, looked incredibly displeased to see Gold Crusher, the muscle giant. He managed to convey a flaming frown, which spoke more of death than displeasure. It was matched by Gold

Crusher's annoyance. Think bristling with testosterone and magnified by a billion.

Infernorator whipped his fiery tentacle toward Gold Crusher in a blur of speed. But Goldie was prepared. His eyes glowed even fiercer as gold lightning arced from them to keep the fire at bay. Supernatural stalemate.

I'd never had a religious upbringing so I felt free to invoke every deity I could think of to show me this was just latent hallucinogens twisting the reality of two men in a simple gang war. Fighting for rights to the woodsy turf.

The creatures extinguished their lights. Apparently they had come to some wordless agreement because both began to scan the forest with eerily identical movements. I pulled myself sharply back behind the tree.

My foot caught on a twig. Its snap seemed to bounce off every tree in a kind of megaphone echo. Hoping against hope that luck was on my side and I hadn't actually been heard, I peeked around the cypress.

Only to find them both staring directly at me.

Flight kicked in again.

"Sophie! Sophie!" I heard Theo bellowing.

I risked a glance over my shoulder. The unexpectedness of his voice had swung the attention of the death twins his way.

I stopped cold. "No, Theo! Run away!"

He didn't. Before you ask, yes, everything did gear down into slow motion in that car crash kind of way. Except a car crash would have been like a Merry-Go-Round ride in comparison.

My eyes widened in horror as Theo came careening into view. The two creatures turned on him.

A look of dread came over Theo's face at the same second that both beings shot off their deadly bursts.

I jumped out from behind the tree. I was pure adrenaline.

Also, rage. I'd been picked on once too often. This attack was off-the-charts unprovoked and unfair. Without any conscious thought, I raised my hands. I felt my anger travel through my body to my palms.

They tingled with it. Burned with it.

Then fury took form as a ribbon of moss green light shot from each of my palms like vines to snake themselves around the creatures, causing their hits on Theo to go wild.

Gold Crusher was lifted like he was nothing. As if my light ribbons had substance. Infernorator's fire was held in check by his bindings.

The ribbons spun faster and faster, engulfing them like a spider entombing its prey for the kill. Dirt, small branches, and rocks were caught up in the fury of its whirlwind. Gold Crusher's and Infernorator's faces were going into psycho old person land.

Then, from one blink to the next, their faces practically skeletal with age, the light constricted, then blinked out of existence. I dropped my hands in horror. The debris dropped to the ground as harmless dirt, with no sign of the beings.

The color drained from my face.

My life as I knew it had ended.

4
Between a Rockman and a hard place
δ′

The phrase "that wasn't supposed to happen yet" did nothing to reassure me. Neither did the fact that my best friend didn't seem upset or surprised by what had just happened. If anything, he looked annoyed.

"Yet?!" I screeched. "You mean it was supposed to happen at some point?"

"Not for another couple of years." Said as if that was going to make everything better.

I took a step toward him, not even aware that my hands were outstretched. "You knew about this?"

Theo lunged at me, grabbing my wrists and lowering my arms. "You may think you want to kill me," he began.

"Not 'think,'" I growled, "know."

"Killing me is not going to get you answers. The Rockman-Bloom alliance must hold." He searched my face intently.

I gave a tight nod and he released my wrists. "Are you even really my friend?"

He gave a derisive laugh. "Sophie, I've walked through

Hell for you. I'm your best friend. Give a boy a chance to explain."

I crossed my arms. "Fine. Go ahead."

He shook his head. "Not here. We have to get you back inside school grounds." Theo took a quick glance around and motioned for me to follow, running back through the woods to the fence.

"Why?" I questioned, trotting after him.

We could hear fire truck sirens approaching. They must have seen the smoke from the attacks. Small brush fires dotted the woods and my eyes were tearing up.

"The school is protected ground. The only place you're truly safe."

"You know this how?" I panted.

"Who do you think protected it?" he retorted, not even slowing.

"Fairies?" I muttered sarcastically, painfully dragging myself back over the fence.

"No such thing."

"Typical. Sparkly winged beings, sorry. Fire throwing ghost, no problem," I said in a slightly higher tone of voice than normal.

"Not a ghost. Though I can see how the flying might have confused …" He peered at me as I emitted a strangled laugh. "You're acting hysterical. You're in shock, right?"

You think? That was such an enormous "d'uh" after what I'd just experienced that I couldn't even dignify it. I stood there, my mouth gaping open and closed like a fish as Theo nodded.

"Yeah," he said, assessing me. "Definitely shock."

I punched him. Hard. It may not have done anything for the shock but it felt good. I spun on my heel and continued through the back field to the school.

"If you're gonna hear me out, you'll have to keep an open mind," he said, jogging after me.

"How could I possibly have to get more open after," I waved my hand back toward the woods, "those things?"

"That's only one small part of it." He held the door open for me and we slipped inside through one of the many sets of heavy glass doors that led into the school.

"Fine. But I want Hannah."

He looked at me, confused. "You sure?"

I shrugged. "Anything you have to tell me, you can say in front of her."

You may be wondering why, given all I was about to hear, I would want Hannah to discover exactly how freaky I was. The answer was simple, boys and girls. Denial ain't just a river in Egypt. It didn't matter that I'd just seen fire fiends and seven-foot-tall lightning men. Or even that I'd shot green pyrotechnics from my hands. I still figured there had to be a rational, logical explanation for all this.

I wanted my best girlfriend there for moral support and to laugh this off when we saw it was all a big misunderstanding.

"You're a goddess," Theo said in a low voice, pulling me aside. He knew me well enough to figure out what I was thinking. "This isn't a joke."

I shook my head so hard, it hurt. "How does that

make any sense? No. You can't expect me to believe that everything I know about my entire life is wrong."

"Explain what happened out there, then." Theo gazed at me with a seriousness I'd never seen from him before. "I need you to believe this."

It was Theo's tone of voice more than anything else, even more than what I'd just seen and done, that forced me to consider wrapping my head around the reality of his words. And yet … "I can't."

I glimpsed Bethany down the corridor as we went hunting for Hannah. She threw me her best glower, which promised retaliation galore.

Huh. If this was real, having the wicked awesome powers of a Supreme Being could rock. I practically salivated at the thought of what I could do to Bethany. I aged her up in my head to horror movie proportions.

Hannah didn't see why we were headed on a secret mission to the gym but she kept quiet until we got there and Theo had closed the doors.

Hannah made herself comfortable on the floor. "What's with the hush hush?"

"I was in the forest," I explained. "And then these *things* showed up to kill me. Except I'm fine. Which is seriously weird since I should be lacking on the living front. But what's really freaking me out?"

"This drug trip you're still on?" she asked.

"I managed to blow the boogeymen into a zillion fragments. One second, I'm scared. Pissed off. The next, I'm the supernova of doom. I've never even been good at sports."

"Huh?" Hannah was understandably confused.

And then it hit me. "Ohmigod. I'm a death machine." I'd just killed two creatures. Yeah, I'd squashed my share of spiders and mosquitos. But these were, okay, if not human, than human-esque. Ish. Did that make me a murderer? "Theo, I don't like this game anymore."

Theo sighed. "It was you or them. Feel sorry for them and it'll be the last feeling you have."

Now I was getting angry. "Then you should have prepared me. Not dumped it on me in a life or death situation, where I get my first kill and then am supposed to be cool with it all. You didn't feel obliged to share until I almost took your head off with my destructo fun. What if I'd killed you?"

Hannah looked between us. "Why are you having a totally nonsensical argument?"

Theo paused, like he wasn't sure where to begin. "My real name is Prometheus."

"And I am Bond, James Bond," Hannah replied in a deep tone of voice.

Theo's reveal triggered a memory of a long-ago English lecture. Not to mention made sense of Cassie's weird mutterings. "I'm Persephone, aren't I?" This begged the question of how Cassie knew but I'd have to get to her later. "Goddess of Nature or something."

"Spring," Theo sighed. "Also, embodiment of earth's fertility."

"Explains her child bearing hips," Hannah quipped. "Spare me the details on how she's supposedly fertilizing the earth."

"Saul," Theo said to Hannah, using his nickname for her (Hannah Solo to Solo to Saul) "we're not kidding."

"Why don't we take this from the top?" Hannah insisted in a firm voice. "You two can tell me the situation and I can decide how big a pair of creeps you're being for playing a lame joke."

"Our story starts back on Mt. Olympus sixteen years ago," he began.

"Nice try," Hannah interrupted. "I may only know Mythology 101 but those gods predated New Kids On The Block."

"Obviously, gods have been around for millennia. Sophie's predicament starts just over sixteen of your earth years ago." He shook his head. "Suppose I better back up."

Hannah frowned. "Suppose you better quit now. Seriously, you two. In what universe did you think I'd fall for this stupid story?"

Unbelievable sure. But stupid? "You don't think I could be a goddess?"

"Less than 'not at all.'"

"Let's see you run," Theo encouraged as if I was a Border Collie.

"Or I could blow Hannah up."

"Hannah isn't ready for advanced goddessing. Baby steps. Run."

Hannah laughed in disbelief. "Set it to expert and go. I'm all eyes."

"Watch and be amazed." I may not have totally come

to terms with this, but that didn't mean Hannah got to doubt me.

I took off, positive I could now push the limits of speed.

Apparently not. I returned to my starting point under Theo's disappointed gaze. "I didn't think it was possible but you're a worse runner than before. I'm not even sure that counted as a slow jog. Guess the goddess is diluted by human," he said.

"Fun as this was, watching Soph jumping around like a constipated elephant, I'm outta here," Hannah said, getting to her feet.

I stopped her from leaving. "You have a divorce lawyer for a dad and a psychologist for a mom. Your entire home life is all about everything that's wrong with people. If you can believe some of those wackjobs' problems, then you can stay here, be my supportive friend, and believe in exactly what's wrong with me right now." I looked around the room, desperate for some way to prove this to her. And, let's face it, me. "Super strength. Let's do that one." I was pretty sure I'd ace any test on that subject.

Theo dragged Hannah across the gym in my determined wake.

I stopped in front of the chin-up bar, wrapped my hands around it and tried to pull myself up. I could barely lift myself off the ground. That couldn't be right. I'd destroyed two supernatural creatures. I would not be defeated by my own body weight.

I narrowed my eyes at the chin-up bar.

At that moment, it symbolized all the feelings of total

uselessness I'd ever felt in gym class. I shot a viney rope out of each hand. I was dimly aware of Hannah gasping but I was more interested in wrapping the vines around the bar and squeezing the crap out of it.

I lifted the bar in the air, my ribbons of light spinning and encircling it. It started to tighten, shrivel, and wither. Then … poof. It was dust.

"Ta da," I gloated. "'Circle of life' can bite me. I. Am. The. Lion. Queen."

Theo didn't look too pleased. I followed his gaze to see that Hannah had fainted.

Before I could figure out what to do for her, Theo "energetically patted" her across the face. Her eyes fluttered open and she glowered at him in indignation.

He shrugged. "You fainted."

We helped her into a sitting position.

"Did you see what she did? Of course I fainted, you idiot!" She stared at me as if I had two heads.

I felt sick. Now that she knew, she'd be all creeped out and not want to be my friend. I didn't want her thinking of me as a monster. "I'm not moving out. So tough." I blurted.

"Uh, yeah. Are you going to be all Jekyll and Hyde now? Do I need to worry about being murdered in my sleep?"

"You're staring at me with this weird look on your face," I insisted.

She smacked my leg. Hard. "You just did this impossible thing that I, of all people, don't believe is possible!" She smacked me again.

"'When you have eliminated the impossible, whatever remains, however improbable, must be the truth,'" Theo added gravely. "Sherlock Holmes," he explained at our stares of bewilderment.

We both smacked him.

"She's a goddess," he said. "Deal with it. Both of you."

I slid to the floor beside Hannah and lay my head on her shoulder.

"Start from the top," she said quietly.

Theo sat down beside us. "Short version? There's this 'mine's bigger than yours' turf war going down between Zeus and Hades. Earth was supposed to stay Switzerland in it. Instead, it became the key battleground and humans suffered. Earthquakes, volcano eruptions, tsunamis, everything you people blame on natural disasters? Not always so natural. Mother Nature and her temper makes a great cover, though."

"And I fit into this how?"

"You're the key to stopping it. The savior of all humanity."

"You're kidding," Hannah said. "No pressure."

I gave a weak laugh. "And to think yesterday, all I had to worry about was Bethany and her yoga zombies."

"How come she never knew this until now?" asked Hannah.

"Yeah. I don't remember being Persephone."

"That's because you weren't supposed to get your memory back in pieces. Upon your eighteenth birthday, the spell that blocked your knowledge of your true self would be undone and it'd all come rushing back. You'd know what to do. And how." He glared at me. "And then that monkey baller Kai kissed you and wrecked everything. As usual."

Whoa. "What does Kai have to do with this?"

"Hades figured that a good way to get back at Zeus was to kidnap his daughter Persephone a.k.a. our bundle of joy, Sophie. But he couldn't risk coming up to Olympus to snatch you. His presence would have set off all kinds of alarms and made him vulnerable, so he sent his son." Theo paused. "Kyrillos. Otherwise known as Kai."

My jaw fell open. "You demon spawn liar," I accused Theo. "Just protecting me from a player, were you?"

"I was," he defended hotly. "You two had more ups and downs than a StairMaster."

"Which I have no clue about because this is the first time you've ever bothered to tell me."

Theo pushed his glasses up his nose. "You wouldn't have believed me if I did."

"Do you even wear glasses?" I spat out.

"You dirty little Hobbit!" Hannah exclaimed. "You smooched your cousin."

I shuddered. "My cousin?" I thought I might throw up.

Theo had the good grace to look sheepish. "Human standards of familial taboos don't apply to the gods. Even so, first cousins can legally marry."

"In the backwoods of Alabama," I groaned. "Just give me a banjo and teach me the 'Deliverance' theme now." I slapped my knee. "Yee haw!"

"Astonishingly melodramatic. Even for you." Hannah shook her head at me.

I pulled my knees up to my chest and wrapped my arms around them. "Fine. Let's just stick with the facts, shall we? My uncle, Lord of Hell, wanted to kidnap me, probably kill me. Does that about sum things up?"

"Hades," Theo corrected, "not Hell. And killing you would have been difficult and painful," Theo assured me. "Immortality and all that."

"Nice try. You can't kill someone who's immortal." Hannah had raised a good point.

"You're confusing immortal and unkillable. Immortal just means you won't die given the natural scheme of things. Not that you can't. And when Immortals kill other Immortals … They like to toy with them first. Break them."

His eyes were bleak as he spoke in a dead voice. "Takes a long time to break an Immortal."

I shot Hannah a confused look. I was missing something here.

Hannah was glowering. I'd seen that particular look of hers before. Usually when she refused to accept a situation. Numerous teachers had been the recipient of that glower.

Then she sighed and dropped her head, with a small shake. "Theo," she prompted gently.

I whipped my head between the two of them. "What? Translate please?"

"If you hadn't fallen asleep in class," Hannah admonished.

"Yeah. Bad Sophie. What am I missing?"

"Theo—Prometheus gave mankind fire and pissed Zeus right off."

"Your liver!" I remembered, shouting at Theo. "Zeus was so mad, he chained you to a rock and made a vulture come by to eat your liver every day." Yikes. The boy knew exactly how long it took to be broken.

Hannah squeezed his hand. Guess she believed him now.

Theo blinked back to attention. "Persephone was immortal. You're human. Doubt it transferred. My bet is you'll reach super old age over full-on living forever."

Theo looked between me and Hannah. I guess between my shell shock and Hannah massaging her temples like she was in pain, he figured we needed to level out. "Sugar and caffeine. Now."

Theo had every staff member wrapped around his finger. Our cook, Ms. Washington, especially adored him as he flirted with her shamelessly. It did get him bakery perks, so the boy was onto something.

He used his charm to score us coffee and chocolate chip peanut butter cookies destined for tonight's dessert. We ate them—as we did every meal—at one of the scarred wooden tables of varying sizes, seated on mismatched chairs.

I picked one up and inhaled its yumminess. "You got peanut butter in my chocolate," I said casually, trying not to show how scared I was. See, Hannah and I had this stupid ritual we always did. And if she didn't answer me, then I knew everything had changed between us.

69

"You got chocolate in my peanut butter," she replied.

I sighed in relief.

"Goof," she said, nudging my leg with hers. "You're not getting rid of me that easily."

Theo added about four packages of sugar to his coffee then continued his tale. "Hades sent Kai to Olympus to kidnap you to see if he could use you as leverage. Plus there was the added bonus of torturing you for any dirt on your dad."

"Delightful," I murmured between bites.

"There was a snag. You and Kai."

"Me and Kai what?" I leaned forward, eager to find out.

Theo sighed. "You fell in love. No one counted on that. Kai stole you away to the Underworld, but he wouldn't let Hades touch you. And it wasn't worth the headache to Hades to cross him, since he had you, for all intents and purposes, as his prisoner. It was all disgustingly nauseating bliss until someone decided to murder Persephone."

So people had wanted me dead before, too? "Who?"

"Must have been Hades," Hannah replied.

Theo shrugged. "Someone wanted you gone. Could have been anyone. Neither Hades nor Zeus wanted you two hooked up. Lesser gods would do anything to win their favor. Suck-ups."

"Dead, though. It seems a little extreme." I shuddered at the thought.

"Sometimes, death is a blessing which we don't have,"

Theo responded darkly. I felt bad for him because after that whole liver thing, he knew what he was talking about.

"What I do know is that I found you, dying on the floor."

"Why were you in Hades? You lived on Mt. Olympus." It seemed very suspicious to me that he just happened to be there. "Also, we need more cookies."

"You've had four," Hannah pointed out.

"I'm having a very trying day. Better pimples than a fiery, mortal death."

Hannah made the motion of playing the world's smallest violin.

"Will you two shut up and let me finish?" asked Theo.

"If you get cookies," I said.

Theo obliged. Probably because he knew I'd just keep whining "Theo, can I have a cookie?" until he did. Smart boy fetched one more small biscuit for each of us.

"Let's just say," he said, breaking his cookie open, "I didn't like constantly running into the god who had caused my liver to keep getting eaten. Zeus is a douche. Of epic proportions. Hades is too but he's all 'the enemy of my enemy is my friend' crap. Otherwise, I'd never have been allowed in. Mr. Paranoia had the Underworld clamped down tight."

"You found Sophie, I mean *Persephone* and … ?" Hannah prompted.

"I spirited her body away. Essentially made a deal to put her soul, her essence into human form."

"Can I have my other body back?"

"No. It's dead."

That fact shouldn't have upset me so much. This me didn't know or remember the other me. But I felt gutted. Like I'd lost someone incredibly close to me. Guess I had.

Theo must have noticed how pale I went at the finality of his words because he added gently, "Sorry. It was the only way."

I grudgingly nodded.

"My plan was to watch over you as you grew up human and then when you were eighteen, release your true identity, train you to your full powers, and let you fight for mankind and end this stupid war." He lit up with the passion of his plan. "Your allegiance is human but your powers are godlike. Since Persephone is Spring and the embodiment of earth's fertility, as both human and goddess, you're bound to the earth. Before you were, *you know*, you told me that you knew the way to stop them. Any memory of that?"

"Nada."

"This plan would definitely anger Zeus," Hannah said, thoughtful.

Theo gave a cherubic grin. "A happy benefit."

"So you were using me."

"I saved you," he retorted.

I thought about this. "You did. But the price was being farmed out to Felicia and then being stuck in this crapshow for pretty much my entire life. If you were really watching over me, you would have pretended to be my nice dad. You wanted me to be your Joan of Arc puppet."

"I couldn't be your dad. Things got ... messed up. That's why you didn't meet me until we were in grade two. Felicia's utter lack of parental ability was perfect because she stashed you somewhere I could keep you safe. Besides, if this had happened the way it should have, you wouldn't be whining."

"Yeah, well, would'a, could'a, should'a," I snarked.

We'd been crossing into one another's personal space. A loud whistle pierced the air. Theo and I whipped around to find Hannah glaring at us.

"Both of you, shut up!"

That startled us. She'd never spoken to us in that tone of voice. The few other students across the room looked over.

"The way I see it," she said more quietly, "it's humans who have been used. If I am going to believe this story, it sounds like we are the only innocent beings in all this. You Greek gods and goddesses are a bunch of narcissistic insensitives with unlimited power. Just a dandy combination."

"Don't lump me in with them," Theo sulked. "I'm a Titan."

"What? You're not even a Greek god?" Oh this was just great.

"Titans are better. We're the deities who came first."

"Theo," Hannah said urgently. She motioned to me. Both of them shot to their feet, grabbed my arms and hustled me out of the cafeteria.

"Look down," Theo hissed at me.

I had no idea what was happening until he shoved me in front of my mirror, back in my room.

"Sweet." My normally blah brown hair had gotten

darker. More lustrous. It had also gone from dead straight to falling in loose ringlets to my shoulders. "I'm like the after picture for a hair ad." Massive delight.

"That's your real color," Theo said. "Persephone's real color."

"Well, it's extreme makeover time because check out her eyes," Hannah said. "They're green. As in brilliant."

Theo looked at me a minute then came to stand beside me. "You're taller too."

"A couple of inches," Hannah agreed.

I glanced down to see my ankles sticking out of my leggings like a total nerd.

Hotter, taller me? My whoop of delight was probably heard in China.

"And I get to live with this now. Thanks," Hannah muttered at Theo.

He gave her a grimace of apology.

"Will my magnificence get cranked to eleven?"

"Only if we're truly blessed," Theo grumbled. "You won't reach your original height, but yeah, it's all part of your true persona. Your natural abilities coming through."

"How big was my rack?" I asked hopefully.

"Such tact," Theo admonished. "I never noticed."

"How would big boobs help you save humankind? Unless you're planning to poke out Hades' eye with your diamond hard nips." Hannah rolled her eyes at me.

"Maybe that was my fiendish plan all along. I am goddess, see me poke."

I gnawed on my thumbnail. The thought that humankind's existence was dependent on me was terrifying. Yes,

I had some new memories and yes, I could do wonderful/awful things, but fundamentally, I didn't feel any different. "It's not like I suddenly feel this deep sense of purpose or destiny or anything."

"You will," Theo assured me. "As more of your memories return."

"Am I going to have to face those … things again?"

"Probably. "

"Things?" Hannah's eyes lit up at the mention of new, potentially deadly creatures. She fell onto her bed, crossed her legs, and got comfy. "Do tell."

Theo flopped himself along the foot of her bed and clued her in. "The Pyrosim are courtesy of Hades."

"I called it an Infernorator." I added my impression. "It reminds me of the dude from 'The Scream' except flying and on fire. Power specialty, shooting fireballs." I squished in between the two of them. I could have sat on my own bed, but I wanted the contact.

"Pyros, from the Greek for 'fire,'" Theo added in a helpful manner. "Villain number two was a Photokia. You know. Photo. Light."

"Gold Crusher. It must play for Zeus?" I glanced over at Theo and got a confirming nod. "Looks like a biker with an overly active growth hormone. Freaky mutation of choice, gold glowing eyes that shoot electricity. Also, thunderbolts tattooed on its head. In case you forget how it's going to destroy you."

I thought about it a moment. "That's lovely. Despite the fact Zeus and Hades hate each other, the one thing they can agree on is that they want me dead. Yay me."

"Think I could get a blood sample from one?" Hannah mused, clasping her hands under her chin.

"No," Theo and I chorused together.

She was not to be put off. She slitted her eyes and regarded me craftily.

"You are not dissecting me." I shoved Theo between us.

"One little blood sample." She threw me her most winning smile. "For science. I bet it would prove very interesting."

"Stand down, Dr. Frankenstein," Theo replied. "Her DNA is human."

"What now?" I asked. I was overwhelmed.

Theo thought about it. "The important thing is to stay within the school grounds at all times. You're back on the radars of Hades and Zeus. We need to keep you safe until you've got all your memories and powers in top form. Don't want you killed before we even get started."

"Look at me, all welcomed back into the bosom of my family." I thought about Bethany and smiled. "No matter. Plenty to make me happy right here."

Hannah peered at me. "That look … I've seen it before."

Theo glanced at me and snorted. "Yeah. In the mirror. It's bloodlust. Magoo," he warned, "whatever you're thinking. No. You don't just get to Godzilla your enemies. You can't let anyone else know who you are. Much as you'd like to, no killing Bethany."

I rolled onto my back and peered at the ceiling

thoughtfully. "What if I just gave her a little anti-face lift? Say in the sixty to eight-five-year-old wrinkle range?"

Hannah shook her head. "Bethany is at least a quarter human and therefore you're bound to protect her."

"But it's okay for a leopard to rip into her."

"Give me that blood sample. If I find any leopard DNA, she's all yours."

"Come on!" I protested. "There've got to be some perks to this stupid destiny."

"We should set some ground rules," Hannah decided. "A code of conduct. Like Dexter has."

"I'm a goddess, not a serial killer. I have no codes."

"Rule number one," Hannah stated, "No hurting humans. You can kill all the mythical creatures you want."

"They're not mythical if they're trying to kill me," I pointed out.

"Don't get uppity with me," she retorted. "Rule number two, I agree with Theo. No blowing your cover. You are strictly Clark Kent around here."

"Couldn't I at least be Tony Stark?"

"Yeah, 'cause that's subtle," scoffed Theo. "If I can pull off a meek exterior, so can you."

I twisted my head to shoot him a skeptical glance. "That's your meek exterior? You're the most sarcastic bastard I know."

"You should hear me when I'm not censoring myself."

"Rule number three," Hannah swung her legs off the bed. "To be determined as I see fit. As are rules four through infinity."

"You can't do that."

"I just did. And there's no point huffing about it. See rule one." She smirked. "You know, now that I've got my head around this, I think I'm going to like this new state of being." She scrunched up her face. "Not like I have a choice. Adapt or die."

Neither, apparently, did I. Sophie Bloom, disaffected adolescent, had a new gig; Persephone, savior of all mankind. All right. That didn't have such a bad ring to it.

There was still one thing I had to do. Hannah and Theo headed down to dinner but I excused myself, pleading a headache. In reality, I just wanted some alone time.

After one more quick mirror check of joy, I cracked my laptop open and began to Google myself. There were a zillion variations on my story. I shied away from the ones involving rape and pomegranates. Rape for obvious reasons and pomegranates because it freaked me out that my love of that fruit might have pre-dated my birth.

I read about how Dad might have been married to Hera but that didn't stop him whoring around with my real mother. Demeter. Which begged the question of where she was, because allowing me to be kidnapped was a serious parenting oversight. Although, almost better than the thought of me kicking Bethany's ass was imagining what my true mother would do to Felicia.

I stared at my screen for a long time, then opened my email and began to type. *Dear Your Royal Imperialness Demeter, Goddess of Grain and Fertility, Preserver of Marriage, and Bringer of Seasons, Or can I just call you Mom?*

You've read the rest of that email, so as you know, I

had nowhere to send it. But boy, did I wish I did. I had a feeling that she was the one person who would tell me the truth.

Of course there was always Kai, but he'd opened this whole can of worms then disappeared. I had no clue where to find him.

If I had been reunited with my girlfriend whom I'd thought was dead, I'd be ecstatic. Kai was furious, which made me think that maybe he hadn't believed I was dead. Maybe he'd been looking for me all this time. That's why he asked me if it was all a big game.

In my opinion, even if he *was* mad that I'd disappeared for sixteen years, he should have come back. If I was his big love, the dummy should have been here kissing me some more. Helping me. Whatever.

God or human, males were stupid across the board.

My stomach growled. Being a goddess sure burned calories. I checked my watch and saw that if I hurried, I still had time to nab some chow. Glancing down at my clothing, I realized that it was dirty from my outdoor encounter. I was dismayed to find that my sweater had gotten badly snagged as well. I briefly considered changing but didn't think I'd have time.

With my hair coming loose from its elastic, I flew down the hallway toward the cafeteria. As I rounded a corridor, I collided hard with a very solid body. I stumbled back, aware of Principal Doucette saying "Here is one of our juniors, Sophie Bloom. Sophie, meet our new transfer student."

I straightened up to find out who had enrolled as our new victim. I mean, student.

There before me was Kai, in faded jeans, slung low on his hips, and a black sweater. His hair flopped over one eye and he had a slight case of dark stubble along his jaw. Apparently, no detail was too small to notice about this guy. If only I could channel that into something useful. Like homework.

Kai gave me the once over and his eyes darkened. With an insolent grin, he stuck out a hand for me to shake. "Pleased to meet you, Sophie," he drawled.

I stared at his outstretched hand and thought about my disheveled hair, dirty clothes, and general unkempt appearance. If I'd ever thought I'd see him again, it would have been wearing something very different. One of those "bet you're sorry you can't have me" outfits. Not a "bet you're glad you don't want me" one.

"Sophie, where are your manners?" Principal Doucette asked.

Gone, I supposed. Along with rules one and two. I was going to wipe that smirk off Kai's face if I had to kill him.

5
Truth is stranger than prediction
ε′

Principal Doucette cleared his throat. "I was hoping you could show Kai around the school."

"Sorry, Principal. I'm late for supper."

"I'll do it," Bethany purred, inserting herself between Kai and me. With a subtle stomp on my toes as a special bonus.

I stepped around her into Kai's eyeline in time to see him brighten.

"Works for me," he told the Principal.

Jerk. Just because I was dead, didn't make me any less his girlfriend, did it? Considering the circumstances of my demise, I was the only one allowed to be in a snit. He should have been Mr. Adoring, kissing me, not Mr. Asshat flirting with another girl. No. No thinking about his kisses. That way lay madness.

"Great. Enjoy yourselves." I stomped off, but not soon enough to avoid seeing Bethany take his arm to lead him away.

Hannah and Theo were still having dinner when I dumped my tray on their table. The cafeteria had the standard buffet set-up complete with classy plastic trays to carry our food.

"More death creatures?" Hannah whispered.

"Worse. Kai is here."

"How?" Theo demanded.

"Beats me. He's our newest transfer student."

Theo swore. I'm guessing in Greek.

"You're really gonna have to teach me some of those. I think they may come in handy," I said. "Bethany has glommed on to him like a parasite."

Hannah craned her neck around.

"You aren't seriously looking for him, are you? That violates all kinds of rules in the best friend handbook."

"I'm curious. You go from not liking any guys to getting all hot and bothered about this one. I'm dying to see the attraction."

"It's not attraction," I retorted. "It's genetic conditioning. Persephone was, so I am too."

"Don't think it works like that," Theo said. "Like it or not, and I don't, your Sophie self is attracted to him on its own."

"No. I refuse to have anything in common with Bethany."

"I'm more interested in the nature of his feelings for you," Hannah said.

I caught sight of them coming our way and scootched down in my seat. "Frak it all," I swore. "Play it cool."

By cool, I meant ignore them. Apparently, I should have detailed it in a memo.

"Hi," Hannah said brightly, forcing Bethany and Kai

to pause by our table. "I'm Hannah Nygard." I kicked her, the traitor.

She shot me a "don't be stupid" look.

"Kai." He slid his gaze over Hannah and Bethany. "You ladies are definitely a sight for sore eyes after the last school I went to."

What was I? Chopped liver? Also, he was a giant liar. Kai had grown up roaming Hades and pestering its inhabitants, gods and dead humans alike, for their knowledge. Hey. Look at me all remembering stuff.

He shook his head sadly and added, "All boys school. We drew lots to see who had to go in drag to the school dances. It wasn't pretty."

Bethany tittered.

"Especially when you stole your dad's wine and kissed that nymph only to discover that she wasn't ..." I trailed off, vaguely remembering that Kai had told me—well Persephone—that story at some point in strict confidence. Underworld Jr. looked thunderous. Theo was highly amused. He fake coughed, trying to cover a laugh.

Kai regarded Theo and stuck out his hand. More in a "take it or I'll kill you" way than in a "nice to meet you" kind of way. "We haven't officially met. Kai."

Theo looked at Kai's hand like it was a snake coiled to strike but reluctantly shook it. "Theo."

Kai's eyes widened at the contact. "Theo, huh?" he mused.

Theo didn't flinch. Or break eye contact. "That's my name," he said.

"Names are so interesting." I said to Kai. "Yours is

Greek, isn't it? I'd love to learn all about where you come from."

Totally ignored. Kai turned his focus back to Hannah. More precisely, to her chest.

Hannah arched an eyebrow as she not-so-subtly cleared her throat.

Kai raised his eyes to hers. "I like a woman with a big …," he pointed at her T-shirt which read "well endowed" over a picture of a giant brain. "… cerebellum."

Hannah leaned forward, seemingly thrilled that he appreciated her science humor. "What's your first class?"

"Biology."

"Me too. We could be lab partners."

Kai nodded. I wondered where this was leading.

"We're studying praying mantises. You know, how the female devours her mate? Just rips the head off." Hannah batted her eyelashes at him. "Maybe you could help me do a live recreation."

That was my girl. Always going in for the kill.

Kai didn't bat an eye. "As long as it involves mating."

What a dog.

"I love Greece," Bethany declared, slow on the uptake, pushing her way firmly back into Kai's attention. "My dad took me there last summer. Beautiful people."

"Not as beautiful as you," Kai replied. He was good.

I failed to suppress a groan.

"We done here?" Bethany asked, shooting me a disdainful stare.

Kai fixed me in his gaze for a split second. "For now," he murmured low enough for only me to hear. I pulled my gaze away from his eyes and found myself staring instead at his full lips and stubbled jawline. For some reason, the sight of this made me very cranky.

"I'll catch you later," Kai promised Theo.

"Knock yourself out," Theo replied.

"Check you out, Bloom," Anil interjected, doing just that. He stopped beside our table and balanced his food-laden tray on one hand. "New hair cut?"

"Something like that," I replied breezily.

Hannah smirked at the wrestler's abrupt switch from hitting on her to hitting on me. "Doesn't she look amazing?"

I scratched the side of my neck, which only Hannah could see, using my middle finger.

"It's a definite upgrade," Anil agreed.

I patted my hair and smiled. "Thanks." Not that I cared about Anil, but all compliments welcome and besides, Kai didn't look too thrilled. Anil gave me a thumbs up and moved on.

"Lead on," Kai directed Bethany, who was only too happy to comply.

"Ugh." Hannah groaned when he left. "You've got to be kidding me."

I stared at her, confused. "You felt nothing at his voice? His eyes? His body?" I fanned myself.

"Penisaurus Rex is not my type," she said. "Could he have hit on me more blatantly? In front of you?"

I cheered up. Best friends were the greatest.

"That was the point," Theo said. "Make Sophie jealous. See how she reacted."

"I was Jack Frost, "I replied. "But speaking of reacting, he made you, didn't he?"

"Yeah."

"Is that going to be a problem?" I wondered.

"Not as long as we don't leave the grounds," Theo assured me. "But the sooner you get your memories back and master your powers, the better."

"Theo," Hannah mused, "why can't you just take up your real form and protect us all that way?"

He shifted, uncomfortable. "I just can't." Abruptly he stood up and carried his tray off.

"Junior year has just gotten much more complicated," Hannah sighed.

Had I any idea how much, I may not have slept as soundly as I did that night.

I awoke on Monday morning ready to face the day. Or, at least, Guidance class. I'd have my ally Ms. Keeper after all.

I stumbled into the room with seconds to spare before the bell and took my seat. Everyone was buzzing about Kai, who thankfully was not in this class. Which I had counted on, my careful attention to my appearance revealing nothing beyond the desire to please myself.

Yeah, I hadn't fooled Hannah earlier, either.

Ms. Keeper entered and shut the classroom door. "Good morning, everyone," she said. "For those of you who haven't met me yet, I'm Ms. Keeper. I'll be replacing Mrs. Rivers."

There was silence for a second as everyone took in the hip, very attractive woman standing in front of them.

"Whoa. Trade up," one of the guys muttered.

Bethany narrowed her eyes at her competition. Which to Bethany was any good looking female in the same room as her.

In my opinion, Keeper totally won that battle.

"I want to start today with an exercise."

"Kegels," guffawed Anil, kicking one of his buddies across the way. I ignored him.

"Now, this is a communications exercise about self-image. I want each person to write down three truths about the others in their group. They should reflect how you see each person. Don't immediately just bash them. Be thoughtful in your comments. They won't be read aloud. Then distribute the comments accordingly."

People were already starting to complain so she held up her hand for silence, keeping it in mid-air until we'd all complied.

"When you get yours," she continued, "I want you to consider those truths and see if they match your perception of yourself. And if not, why not? You will have to hand in a written summary of the differences or perhaps, things that were in agreement." She put us into small groups of three.

I considered my group. Cassie, me, and Bethany. Delightful. Gee, could this have anything to do with Keeper wanting me to speak up about Bethany? Was she thinking she'd arranged a safe venue for that?

While it felt good to have someone trying so hard to be in my corner, I would never have ratted Bethany out. The Bethanys of this world always landed on their feet.

And my life would have gotten worse, not better. It was all irrelevant now, anyway.

What to write then for this flake fest assignment?

Felicia had once dated some guru and I'd spent a summer putting up with "positive language" and "I statements" which was all fine and good but didn't do much to hide the fact that he was a hypocrite who was cheating on his wife with two other women and had a not-so-secret drug problem. Wheat germ didn't disguise the smell of pot. Oh well. I could play this game.

Bethany leaned over and hissed, "Fake contacts and a dye job aren't going to help. Kai is out of your league, junior."

Even if I couldn't actually kill her, I could think about it. In great detail.

I sighed. No time for fun right now. I leaned over to Cassie. "Can we talk later?" As in, you're going to share why you knew who I was.

Cassie, skittish, opened her mouth to speak but—

"No talking, girls."

Cassie turned her attention back to her paper, looking like she'd just dodged a bullet. I'd corner her after class.

I considered the assignment.

Might as well get the hard one over first. I regarded Bethany from under my lashes, then wrote, "you project confidence." Because bullies projected confidence. Confidence that they were going to beat you down. Next I went for "you lack interpersonal skills." See the previously mentioned bullying.

I watched Bethany twirl a lock of hair around her

finger as she thought. She caught me looking and in one fluid motion disentangled her digit and flipped me the bird. Ah-ha! "Your motor skills are admirable." There. Nothing that could get me in trouble and even all true.

Cassie was tougher but I managed to find three "truths" for her as well. Then Ms. Keeper called time and had us exchange our papers.

Bethany's observations about me were concise. "Short. Stupid. Suck." I looked up from the note to see her smirking at me. "Got three for you," I said softly. "Giant, gelatinous, glutes." I left her working it out.

A second later a wadded up paper ball hit my head. Guess she'd gotten it.

I unfolded the "truths" Cassie had written about me. "A girl of exceptional power." O-kay. Next one. "Confused about her true self." This was getting creepy. Her desk was empty so I scanned the room to see where she'd gone. She was having a quiet but intense conversation with Ms. Keeper.

Ms. Keeper seemed to be patiently trying to calm Cassie down while Cassie kept shaking her head "no." Keeper saw me watching and gave a small smile, trying, I guess, to let me know Cassie would be all right.

I returned to the last truth that Cassie had written. "The instrument of our destruction." I dropped the note like I'd been scalded.

Excuse me? Destruction? I was supposed to save humans, not destroy them. Unless ... is that how I was planning on stopping the war? Just destroy earth? Theo never actually said I had a way to save everyone. Just stop the war. I swallowed hard to keep the nausea from rising in my throat. I was really going to have to start carrying around some Tums.

Also? What the hell? How could she have known any of this? I hadn't even been clued in until yesterday. So was Cassie in on it too? But then why didn't Theo mention her?

My hands were trembling. Terrified that I was going to do something inadvertent, like freak and take out the second floor, I shoved them under my butt.

I had to talk to Cassie. But when I checked back at Ms. Keeper's desk, she was gone. I figured she must have gone to the washroom, but she never returned.

I had no idea what else was discussed in class that day. I was a giant ball of nerves, staring at the clock and dying for the bell to ring so I could talk to Theo. Or find Cassie. Or do something resembling anything to figure out what was going on.

The shrill bell indicating end of class had never been so welcome. I grabbed the piece of paper with Cassie's "truths" on it, shot out of the classroom, and barreled my way down the hallway to my English class, which I had with Theo and Hannah.

I slid onto the low couch next to Theo and shoved Cassie's "truths" at him. "Explain this," I hissed. Hannah dropped her books on the sofa arm next to him and peered over his shoulder to read it.

He blankly returned it to me. "No clue."

"Did you see the part that said 'destroyer?'"

"Yes."

"Am I gonna blow up the earth?"

"It wasn't part of my plan but since everything is screwed, anything is a go."

"Was it part of my plan? I told you I could stop the war. Not save humanity. Was this how I meant to do it? Was I some kind of human racist?"

Theo thought about it. "No. I don't know. Maybe? You do get extreme about your likes and dislikes."

Hannah snorted. I ignored her.

"For the one person who is supposed to know what the deal is, your intel sucks."

He stared at me in distaste. "Don't like what I got? Find a new source. Sixteen years of planning just went out the window. I'm not sure it's worth the bother."

"Hey!" Hannah protested. "Human being. Sitting right here."

I patted her hand reassuringly. "What's the skinny on Cassie anyway? She's not part of our wacky gang? Venus, maybe? Or Diana?"

"Obviously not either, since they're the fake names those pretender Romans gave us. Get your gods right," he snarked.

"Listen Rockman, I'm a pissed off teen with unstable powers. You really want to discuss semantics with me?"

The bell rang. "Thank God," Hannah muttered.

Our teacher, Mr. Locke, launched into some diatribe on *Romeo and Juliet*. Luckily, I was an expert at tuning him out while appearing to pay rapt attention so I could focus on the important matter at hand. Namely, me.

I tapped my pen anxiously against my leg. Hannah

plucked it from my grasp to write in Theo's binder. *Could Cassie be from Olympus and you don't know?*

Theo shook his head and wrote *I'd know if anyone from Olympus was on school grounds. Talk. To. Cassie.*

I tilted his binder so I could reply. *If I can find her. Took off during class. Didn't return. Left all her stuff.*

Hannah read it and turned a worried look on me. I nodded, which Mr. Locke fortunately took as agreement with whatever long-winded point he'd been making. He smiled at my enthusiasm. I felt a twinge of guilt. I seriously hoped I wasn't planning on obliterating him.

Lunch period found me too keyed up to eat. I raced around the school searching for Cassie and eventually found her in the sick bay. Okay, Nurse Hamata's office. I just called it a sick bay because in the sci-fi version of my life—Crap. This was the sci-fi version of my life.

Cassie was lying on one of the two beds in there, with the lights off. I checked to make sure there was no one else around, then crept softly over to her bedside.

"Cassie?" I said quietly. "We need to talk."

"Go away," she moaned.

"What's wrong? Can I get you something?" She was holding her head and rocking so I flung open the cabinets looking for a Tylenol.

"The blood," she cried.

I froze. "Cassie. Are you talking about me?"

Nothing. I put my hand on her shoulder and she began speaking super rapidly. Some stream-of-consciousness stuff.

"OneaboveonebelowakeyawakeitisnomoreITISNO-MORE ..."

"What? Slow down?"

She thrashed, bucking off the bed. I stumbled back.

"What's going on here?" I whirled around. It was Ms. Keeper, looking every inch the staff member who'd just caught a student where they shouldn't be.

"There's something wrong with her."

She ran her hands through her hair, making tiny purple spikes. "Cassie is ill, Sophie. I'm getting her help. But I'm sure she wouldn't want you to see her like this." She had taken hold of my shoulders and was steering me toward the door.

"I guess not," I agreed, trying to get one more look at her. But Ms. Keeper had ushered me into the hallway. She paused at the doorway. "Do you think Bethany has been bullying Cassie as well?"

"I don't think so."

"I just worry because Cassie is the kind of girl that Bethany could easily boss around. Don't you think?"

Quiet, not many friends, a little weird. "Yeah. I guess she is."

She nodded and shut the door.

I slid down the wall and tried to memorize the gibberish that Cassie had spouted, so I could share it with Hannah and Theo and see if they understood it. I sure didn't. But that didn't keep it from sounding bad. Really bad.

I didn't see Hannah and Theo again until after classes were done for the day. I'd skipped out and spent the afternoon in the library doing more research, typing what she'd said into every search engine I could think of. No results. I didn't actually think it was going to be that easy, but jeez, something could have come up.

I pulled the two of them into an empty classroom and recited what Cassie had said.

"None of it means anything to you?" Hannah asked.

"Nothing. 'One above and one below' could be me and Kai or Zeus and Hades. Though I couldn't find any reference to Persephone, I mean me, and a key."

"Kai? He's part of the plan?" Theo was radiating thundercloud.

"Maybe?" I idly spun a globe which sat on top of a low bookcase. "Cassie knew I was Persephone. She could be right about this."

If anything, his expression grew darker. "Cassie. She's Cassandra. As in the oracle Cassandra who could predict the future—"

"But who no one believed," Hannah finished. "How did she end up here? This sudden epidemic of Greek figures in teen bodies is a little too *Invasion of the Body Snatchers for me.*" She tilted her head and regarded the chemical equation on the board.

Theo muttered a few more choice words about Kai before answering. "I don't think that's it. Cassandra had a couple kids who everyone figured were murdered. But it's not like there was DNA evidence to prove anything, was there? I think this Cassie is a descendent with the same abilities."

"Could be," I said. "She's always seemed kind of, well, off. I probably do too, now. The stench of crazy."

"What I'm more concerned about is when did she realize all this about you? Could it have been before the kiss?" asked Theo, leaning against a table.

"I doubt it. I never got that sense," I replied. "I'm pretty sure it was that same night. The next morning she made this Persephone reference which I didn't get until you told me your real name. She seemed really wigged out. Mentioned she'd had a bad night."

"I'll bet." Hannah said. "Especially if it was the first time she actually got these predictions or whatever they are for her." She moved up to the board, picked up a piece of chalk and made an adjustment to the equation.

"I tried to ask her about it but we got interrupted. Not that she looked willing to talk."

"Could be when you broke through to your true identity, it triggered her full-on abilities. Which means that she's right and Kai could be integral to all this. You're sure you don't remember anything about the plan?" Theo looked at me hopefully.

"Not yet. Sorry."

"Let's see if she's up for a bit of a chat," Hannah said, brushing chalk dust off of her hands. We walked in silence to the nurse's office. The door was open and the lights were on. Cassie was still there, sitting up on the bed with her back to us.

Theo, Hannah and I exchanged glances. This seemed more promising than before.

Hannah stepped forward. "Cassie?" she said. No response.

I was chilled. This is what had happened last time before the crazy kicked in. I wasn't up to hearing any more doom.

"Cassie?" Theo spoke a little louder. We came around the bed so we could see her. Cassie was staring blankly at a wall.

"She's stoned out of her tree," I said. I shook her but she didn't even react, she was so looped out.

"It's like she's frozen," Hannah commented, waving a hand in front of her face.

Theo picked up a small pill bottle on the table beside her and peered at the label. "Chlorpromazine."

Hannah frowned. "That's an antipsychotic." She took the bottle from Theo. "And a really high dosage of it."

"No wonder she's all zombie," I said.

"This much can't be good for her," Hannah observed. "But I can't tell who prescribed it."

"Someone who doesn't want her speaking, obviously," said Theo. "She might spill something that someone wants kept from Sophie."

"Worse than I'm going to destroy the world?"

"It might not be about the earth," Hannah added. "It might be personal to you." She glanced at Theo. "Like Kai?"

"Prime suspect number one."

"Because you don't like him," I sputtered. "Doesn't mean he'd OD Cassie. That's just evil."

"Or self-serving," Theo pointed out.

"What do we do about her?" Hannah asked, concerned, trying to catch Cassie as she fell slowly backward onto the bed. She lay Cassie down and put a blanket over her.

"We take the bottle and leave her. For now." Theo ordered. "Tonight we come back and see if she's more coherent."

Hannah pocketed the pill bottle. "Fine."

We cleared out of the room in time to find Kai heading straight for us. "Don't you dare abandon me," I muttered to Hannah and Theo.

"Don't panic. All is well," Theo soothed, grasping my elbow and steering me down another corridor before our two parties could actually meet. He pushed us all into a classroom, then peered out of the window to see if Kai had followed.

"That's odd," he said. "He's not coming."

Hannah's hand flew to her mouth in exclamation. "What if he was coming for Cassie, not looking for Sophie? And we just left her alone?"

She flung the door open and we raced back to the nurse's office. The door was locked. I tugged desperately on it to no avail. "Find Stan," I cried. "He has a key."

Hannah and Theo raced off in different directions to track him down while I uselessly pounded on the door. "Cassie? Kai? Open up in there."

It felt like forever but was only moments before Hannah dragged Stan over and he unlocked the door for us.

We bolted inside. But it was too late.

Cassie was gone.

6
If you play with fire, you're gonna get spurned

ς'

"How could he possibly leave with her?" I demanded. "I was outside the door the entire time."

Theo had arrived in time to hear this. "There's always the window."

Hannah looked at him in scorn. "He dragged her limp body out a window?"

Theo cast a cautious look at Stan, waiting patiently for us by the door, before whispering "Not your ordinary guy."

Hannah rushed to the window to look out. "No sign."

"You kids finished?" Stan asked.

We nodded and shuffled out so Stan could lock up.

"I'm going to check her room," Hannah said. "Maybe she came to and decided to head up while we were in the classroom."

"You don't genuinely think that, do you?" asked Theo.

"No," she sighed. "But it's better than the alternative."

"Right. Off we go." He turned to me. "Coming?"

"No. I know it's probably pointless but I'm going to search the school."

Theo clapped my shoulder in encouragement and departed with Hannah.

I spent a good hour roaming around, checking out classrooms and asking students if they'd seen her. No luck.

Frustration overwhelmed me. Not to mention guilt that somehow my awakening as Persephone had inadvertently caused Cassie to come to harm.

Where could she have gone? If I'd been standing outside the door, then the only way out was through the window.

I headed outside to check the ground underneath, in case there were any clues. Footprints, tracks from a wheelbarrow in which her body had been dragged away. It was probably a little too Scooby Doo but I was desperate.

There were marks around the low hedges in the flowerbed but they weren't proof of anything. I sighed and stepped over a bag of fertilizer left on the ground. Pictures of bright, tropical flowers adorned the package.

Flash! I saw myself cavorting in a meadow of the same flowers, which was so pathetic I wanted to puke. Apparently, though, this is what goddesses did for fun. As long as I wasn't fertilizing anything, I could deal.

My head was getting that lovely splitting open sensation again. No way was I going to space out down memory lane in public and risk looking like I was having a seizure. I needed to get somewhere private.

I ran blindly into the school, barely able to see anything in the here-and-now as more memories assaulted me.

The sun had been shining, hot and bright. I could feel it heating my skin through the layers of my filmy gown.

I gazed down upon my body.

Man, I'd been fine. Stupid Theo could have at least made sure I stayed the equivalent level of hotness.

The air was perfumed with grass and a bouquet of floral aromas which should have been cloying but instead seemed to fuel me. I dug my toes into the cool earth. Because I actually was on earth. Somewhere tropical and lush. There was an almost overpowering scent of jasmine.

I nearly collided with the wall in my haste to find somewhere private. There was a girls' bathroom here. If I could just get inside.

Further along, people strolled and children played but I knew they couldn't see me unless I wanted them to. And I wanted to remain invisible. To enjoy the freedom of being alone.

Things were so tense on Olympus. Zeus was always in a rage and everyone was terrified of setting him off. My mother was anxious because …

The thought was elusive. There was something important that I needed to remember. But it wouldn't come. I drifted back to that day.

I got a prickling feeling like I was being watched. Could someone have followed me? I'd tried to be careful but I had nowhere near all the tricks of some of the other gods.

I pivoted slowly and then I saw him. An impossibly gorgeous figure, radiating power.

No. No more Mr. Tall, Dark, and Brooding. I tried to shake it off but like it or not, this was the memory

I was stuck with. Fine. I fast-forwarded to Kai moving into the light. My first look at him. The version of Kai I saw in my memory looked like a taller, more powerful, and slightly older version of the Kai here at Hope Park.

There was only one god he could be. Kyrillos, son of Hades. I'd heard of him but had never seen him. "Kyrillos," I said, in a cool voice.

He gave me a mocking bow. "Persephone."

"What business have you here?"

He padded toward me slowly, like a jungle cat I'd seen in my travels, lithe and dangerous. I refused to be cowed and held my ground.

He examined me slowly and smiled. "My father neglected to speak of your beauty."

He overwhelmed me. I didn't like it so I turned to leave.

He caught me in an iron grip and made me face him. "Not so fast, Goddess." He traced my jawline with one finger.

I suppressed the tremor I felt inside.

"It pains me to do this." He raised his hand and ...

Crack! My eyes startled open.

"That must have been some dream," Kai said. I realized the noise had been him shutting the door of the girls' bathroom. "You were stumbling around. Zoned out. Figured I'd better bring you in here to make sure you didn't kill yourself before you came to."

It was kind of disorienting to see Kai in this utilitarian bathroom when I'd just been thinking of him outside in the tropics. "You hit me," I accused.

"Huh?"

"The first time we met. You hit me and kidnapped me."

I yanked a paper towel out of the plastic dispenser and blotted my forehead.

"I don't hit girls," he scowled.

"I wasn't a girl. I was a goddess. Am a goddess. Stop ignoring the point." Annoyed, I wadded the towel into a ball and threw it in the trash.

"I didn't hit you either, Goddess."

"Cut the crap. I remember. You raised your hand and …" I trailed off.

He snorted. "I raised my hand and you attacked me." He pointed to a tiny silver scar under his left eye. "Gave me that. Nearly lost an eye trying to get you down to Hades."

That could have been the truth. But of course a kidnapper would deny using force. It was another reason to be wary of him. I felt I should keep my suspicions to myself. For now. "Sorry for the inconvenience," I sneered.

He shrugged. "It was kind of hot."

"Oh brother." I rolled my eyes. "Don't tell me you get off on kinky foreplay."

He cocked an eyebrow. "Don't you remember?"

"I am not having this conversation with you."

"Apparently, you are," he replied, smugly.

I had to change the subject because there was no way I could spar with him about sex when I had no idea what had or had not ever happened between us. What if I liked being restrained and screamed like a banshee? What if I turned into a banshee? You could see my dilemma.

I cast around for a safe topic. "Cassie!" I sputtered. "What did you do with her?"

He looked blank. "Who?"

"Cassandra. The oracle?"

"Cassandra is dead. Do you have an actual clue about anything?"

"Not *the* Cassandra. My Cassandra. Cassie. My schoolmate. You were headed toward the nurse's office—"

"Looking for you. Who took off to avoid me."

"Giving you the chance to go get her and spirit her off," I said.

"Why?"

"So she wouldn't tell me that thing."

"What thing?" He sounded genuinely confused. But he could have been a really good actor.

"I don't know. You stopped her before she could tell me."

Kai swore. "You don't make any sense. You pretend to be Bethany coming to meet me. Then you get mad. Kiss me."

"You kissed me first," I pointed out. "Being all insufferable and arrogant."

"Arrogant? That's hilarious. You're the one who let me think you'd been gone all these years having met some horrific fate, when really you've been here playing dolls with Prometheus."

"You said 'gone.' Not 'dead.' You thought I was alive, didn't you?"

"I couldn't believe you were dead," he grudgingly admitted. "It never felt right."

"Is that why you came here? You were looking for me?"

I slid myself onto the cool, blue flecked counter and waited.

"Don't flatter yourself. I figured if you'd been gone this long, you wanted to stay gone. It was brought to my attention that some random school was incredibly warded up. I wanted to know why."

He leaned in close and fixed me in his gaze. "Want to tell me what the past sixteen years were all about?" he asked in a low and deadly tone.

"Not really," I answered, since I couldn't. "I want to know what you did with Cassie."

"Nothing. If I'd wanted to do something to her, you'd never have seen me coming. When you so rudely ignored me, I turned around and left."

"And followed me here."

He laughed. A sound so hollow it practically sounded painful. "I don't need to follow you, Goddess. Ever since we kissed, you've been this burning GPS in my head. I know where you are every second."

I preened, liking that idea.

"It's driving me nuts and I want it to stop."

So much for that. "I thought I was supposed to be the big love of your life."

"I don't even know you," he retorted.

I stared up at the overhead florescent light and shook my head, willing patience. "Nice attitude."

"You're not Persephone. Just some human."

I stood up, making sure I postured myself into full height. "First off, it's a species not a disease. I'm not going to infect you. Second, I am Persephone. You know it. That's why you said 'finally' before you kissed me. I'm Persephone and I'm Sophie."

"How?" he demanded.

"Theo put me in this form to keep me safe."

"From who? How much do you remember?"

"Why? Got something to hide?"

"Not as much as you," he retorted.

We glared at each other for a moment before he abruptly changed the subject. "They're after you now, you know."

"I know. I saw them."

"Zeus and Hades?" He sounded incredulous.

"No. Gold Crushers and Infernorators."

His brow creased in puzzlement.

"Right, not the technical terms." I scrambled to remember what Theo had called them. "A Pyrosim and a Photokia."

"And you escaped?"

"I destroyed them. You might want to remember that as you continue to piss me off."

"It's impossible. You're human," he retorted.

"And a goddess. Get with the program."

He was really getting under my skin. Maybe I just wanted one others person from my past firmly in my corner in the present. Or maybe I'd ingested too much romantic garbage from the movies, but his lack of overwhelming joy at my appearance rankled.

"So you have your powers?" Kai sounded doubtful.

Jerk. My palms started to tingle. I raised my hands. Nothing happened.

Kai crossed his arms across his chest. Totally unconcerned.

I turned my palms over to check them out. They seemed fine.

I refused to let him headtrip me. I was so going to strangle him with my trusty weapons. Yeah. Not what happened. Stupid defective hands.

"Behold: nothing!" he pronounced.

I deflated. "That went well."

Kai's lips quirked. "Out of curiosity, did you think it was going to go better or worse?"

I skewered him in a "not funny" glare. "I don't get it. I smooshed those things. And I was able to show Hannah what I could do."

"I believe you," he replied.

"You do?" It was the last thing I expected from him.

"Yeah. That is your power, after all. And since you wouldn't know about the Pyrosim and Photokia if you hadn't seen them, you must have destroyed them to survive."

"Why didn't it work here, then?" I asked.

"Your little friend Prometheus didn't fill you in?"

I glared at him, not wanting to implicate Theo in anything. Not to Kai, anyway. If Theo was keeping stuff from me, we'd have that out later.

"You haven't been outside since, have you?" Kai motioned to the small frosted window, set high in the wall.

"Not for long. But I don't see how that matters."

"You need to recharge. You're Spring. You're tied to nature and the outdoors. Like the ultimate solar battery."

"So my crummy power has conditions? Figures."

"Even Superman had Kryptonite. Besides, fresh air is good for you."

I took a deep breath and blurted out before I could think twice, "So where does this leave us?"

Kai stared at me, then shrugged. "Wish to Hades I knew. I'll see you around, Sophie Bloom." Then he left.

That was highly unsatisfying. Which seemed to be the tone of all our encounters. While he certainly wasn't chatty about why he was here at Hope Park, I did believe him about Cassie. About the fact that if he wanted to harm someone, they wouldn't know until it was too late. And he wouldn't be caught. I filed that piece of info away under "up the security threat of this guy to DEFCON 2."

My concentration was shot so I headed back to my room. Theo and Hannah were waiting for me.

"She's gone." Hannah was visibly upset. "Her room-mate, Jessica, said that when she returned to her room after class, Cassie's stuff wasn't there. Ms. Keeper was waiting for her to tell her that Cassie's parents had come to get her and that Cassie was being hospitalized for a nervous breakdown. She won't be here for the remainder of the term."

"Jessica didn't believe it, did she?"

"She wasn't sure what to believe." Theo said. "She saw Cassie leave class and couldn't understand what else it could be. Why would Ms. Keeper lie about it?"

"That's the million dollar question." I frowned. "Ms.

Keeper appears and Cassie disappears? It's too much of a coincidence. We need to find out more about this woman."

"The timing sucks," Theo agreed.

"You think it's related?" Hannah asked.

"I'm not willing to chance it," he replied.

"But you said you'd be able to tell if anyone from Olympus was here," I retorted.

"This goes way beyond Olympus. I had no idea Kai was here until you told me. Thing is, how did she get past the wards on this place?"

"Kai did," Hannah pointed out.

Theo shook his head. "The wards keep out anyone intending to cause Sophie physical harm. And encourage Sophie to stay in. Whatever brought Kai here, it wasn't to hurt Sophie."

"Unless we count head games," I muttered.

"Head games won't get you killed unless you leave school grounds," Theo replied. "My guess is he's on a recon mission to learn what happened and report back."

"At which point he'll try to kidnap me again?" Was I going to have to constantly look over my shoulder?

"Not if you stay within school grounds, he can't."

"Let's reason this out," Hannah said. "If Ms. Keeper isn't here to hurt Sophie, then what? Especially since the only one who may have come to harm is Cassie?"

"We have to draw her out," I said. "It's the only way."

"Absolutely not." Theo was adamant. "We don't want a total cockup. Nothing happens until we know why she's here. If she's even a problem. We don't want to tip our hand that we're on to her."

I couldn't believe what I was hearing. "I should just sit here and do nothing? Cassie could be killed."

"Whatever has happened to Cassie is most probably done. We will get to the bottom of this."

There was about as much a chance of me being patient as there was of me winning the Miss America pageant. Actually, if I'd still had my original body, then the odds would have been on me wearing that crown. I had to take action. Goddesses didn't just sit there. What was the point of being a deity if all I did was dance around in meadows?

I needed to use myself as bait and see if I caught a Counselericus Evilicus. The only question was how?

The answer came to me the next day. Even though he'd only been at Hope Park two days, Kai had become the flavor of the month. I sat on the bleachers during lunch, watching him play soccer with some guys in the grass center of our track.

It was difficult to tell who was trying harder to impress him, the jocks on the field or the girls on the sidelines. The more impervious he remained, the more they fell all over themselves.

It surprised me that certain guys were trying to gain Kai's favor. Like the husky Jackson Birt. Jackson might have resembled a grizzly, but he was definitely not smarter than your average bear. His motor skills sucked, too. Brother should have stuck to feats of brute strength because watching him attempt to juggle the ball from foot to foot was just embarrassing. Although perhaps less so than Veronica Chen scooting around to remain in Kai's line of sight at all times. The highlight being when she elbowed Bethany in the head. I grinned just as Kai suppressed his own and caught my eye.

Even from this distance, I felt the chemistry crackle between us. Until he ruined it by looking abruptly away and bestowing a crooked grin of sympathy on Bethany.

Kai didn't count as human so Hannah's rules didn't apply. I could get him alone and ...

That was it! I would go outside, alone at night, and do some training. Unleash my power. If Ms. Keeper was here because of me, she'd be bound to come and check it out. Especially with me all vulnerable and by myself. It made perfect sense to me.

I heard a burst of female laughter and glanced over at the group of popular kids. Given the way Bethany, Veronica, and a couple of other girls were staring at me, a crack had obviously just been made at my expense.

I consoled myself by imagining acts of horrible retribution, while I thought more about my plan.

I didn't say a word to Theo and Hannah. They'd just forbid it or want to come with me and I couldn't take that risk. Hannah was human and as such, killable. For all intents and purposes, Theo was as well. I doubted he had any powers. Given how many times he must have wanted to kill me over the years, the fact that I was still standing had to be evidence of his lack of super power, not his abundance of will power. Because had I been

Theo, I sure would have blasted me on more than one occasion.

And while I probably was killable too, at least I had powers and a fighting chance.

I snuck out after bed check in warm, loose clothes. I decided to practice as far away from the school as possible while still staying on the property. It put me back where I'd seen Kai that first night.

As soon as I got outside, I had an uncontrollable urge to take off my shoes. Even hypochondriac fears of frostbite couldn't keep me from being in bare feet. The grass was cool and ticklish between my toes. I wiggled them deeper, needing to be as close to their roots as possible.

I ran over to a maple tree that still bore a few leaves and pulled a branch down, rubbing the leaves gently across my face. Had I been asked last week, I would have chosen the city over the country, hands down. Now, my nature girl tendencies were going from zero to a billion. Every little detail about the outside fascinated me, from the lone calls of owls, to the texture of bark.

Focus. I had the rest of my life to satisfy my new passion. Now I had to draw Ms. Keeper out so I could discover Cassie's whereabouts and rescue her.

Time to see if I could blast light without have the poo scared out of me. Come to think of it, time to get a cool name for my power. Hmm. Ribbons of Death? Binders? Stranglers? I'd work on it. Meantime, I raised my hands and focused.

Half an hour later, I was sweaty and the only thing I'd achieved was a headache. No one had shown up. My palms remained dazzle-free. I felt like an idiot. I decided to give it one last try and then call it a night. Maybe Theo and I could break into the school office tomorrow and see if they had a file on Ms. Keeper. Yeah, guess that should have been step one.

Instead of concentrating with every ounce of intensity I possessed, I decided to stay relaxed. It worked. Presto. Two moss green beams about fifteen feet long flew from my palms, dancing like ribbons in the wind.

I did it. Thunderous applause and Nobel Peace prize for saving humanity, please. I experimented with moving the light to the left and the right. It was no harder than using a joystick. I sang a catchy little tune about my light ribbons. "Move them to the left, then I move them to the right. I'm an ass-kicking superfreak, I'll do it all night."

Let me be a lesson to you, kids. There is a reason you shouldn't get all cocky. Because if you do, the universe will come along and kick your ass hard.

One minute, I was feeling all smug about my powers, the next, I caught sight of about a dozen Infernorators hovering just outside the fence like a firing squad. Yikes! I froze in terror as they advanced en masse toward me, reaching out their flaming tentacles.

Bless Theo and his wards. Their fire simply bounced harmlessly off the air above the fence. I really was in a giant protective shield. I smiled, thinly. My turn. I figured that since I had the upper hand, I should take these things out.

In my defense, it never even occurred to me that this

was a two-way ward. In my head, it was all about me, me, me. So of course I'd be able to fire outwards.

Yeah … no. I sent my ribbons lashing out toward those bad boys. They hit the invisible shield at full speed, then bounced off it to rebound back at me.

That was the point at which I totally forgot how to control them and just yelped, wildly waving my hands around as I ducked and bobbed and tried not to trip over my own superpower.

A low laugh penetrated my fear. I glanced over, wide-eyed, to see Kai smirking from over by the back fence. For a second. The smirk quickly disappeared as I sent the creepers directly for him.

I will swear on a stack of bibles or whatever that I didn't mean to take him out. It was instinctive. Better him a target than me.

"Duck!" I yelled feebly. He just glowered at me and put out his hand to stop them in their path. I might have felt like a busted bottle of Silly String, shooting these puppies out willy-nilly, but it was pretty impressive the way Kai had them twisting in place like that.

I stood there gaping until he growled, "Quit it" and I snapped back into action. I dropped my hands but that didn't seem to blink the vines out of existence.

"Hurry up!" he snapped, the strain of holding them at bay wearing on him.

Honestly, I had no clue what to do. I tried to shoo them away from him. Less than successful. I only managed to redirect one toward a small sapling, which I then uprooted and used to conk him on the shoulder.

"Of all the useless …" he began.

"Who asked you to show up, anyway?" I shot back. Especially with me once again looking like Grimy, the eighth dwarf. I did the only thing I could think of at that point. Since I'd called the ribbons up with my energy, maybe I could draw them back in. I concentrated on pulling them back into me.

It worked. They dissipated in a rush. Their power flooded inside of me and knocked me back about twenty feet.

I landed like a rag doll. The wind was knocked out of me. I fluttered my eyes open several minutes later to find Kai frowning.

"That was stellar," he commented. "Zeus and Hades won't have to kill you. You're a walking suicide mission."

At the reminder of my nemeses, I turned my head back toward where the Infernorators had been.

"Forget it. The Pyrosim are gone," he said, rubbing his shoulder.

"You okay?"

"The tree didn't help."

"Oops. Sorry. You hid it well," I said.

"I'm a god. I don't show weakness. Around you," he added, "that seems to be a survival skill."

"Ha ha. Next time I'll try and warn you if I'm getting ready to sprout. We could have a hand signal. I'll bet the gods have great hand signals."

"No." Kai crossed his arms. End of discussion.

Or changing of subjects. "Why are you here?" I demanded, refusing his help as I struggled to sit up.

"I told you. Your whereabouts flash in my head."

"No. Here. Hope Park. What do you want?"

"Answers. Why did you disappear on me?"

"Someone tried to hurt me. Maybe it was you."

"It wasn't me," he stated darkly.

"Whatever. Theo didn't know what fate was in store for me so he got me out of dodge."

"And you believe him?"

"Do you have a better explanation for all this? Two days ago, I had no idea who I really was. Theo sure wasn't thrilled to learn what happened when you kissed me."

Kai smirked. "It was my kiss that set this off?"

"Yes. You're very manly. Good for you."

"I think it's good for you," he insisted.

Then he kissed me.

I knew I shouldn't have let him just toy with me and call the shots whenever he felt like it, but he was right there and I've never been very good at denying myself treats sitting in front of me. Believe me, he tasted way better than chocolate.

"Problem is, we don't even like each other," I said when I came up for air.

"I liked Persephone just fine. Since you're looking more like her, I'm willing to ignore the Sophie part." He kissed me again.

I let him. For a minute. That whole lack of willpower thing. Then I stomped on his foot. Hard.

"I am Sophie, you jerk," I finally said. "If you do care for some part of me then prove it."

"I just did." Arrogance oozed off him.

"Please. You probably get turned on by a rock." I shook my head in total exasperation. "What did I ever see in you? You're utterly despicable."

He clenched his jaw slightly and gave a bored shrug.

"Why are you here, Kai? And don't just say answers. You know I don't have them."

"Maybe I have a vested interest in hanging around until you do," he stated cryptically.

"You're a fabulous conversationalist," I fumed.

"I will tell you one thing. Zeus and Hades are furious that you've reappeared in human form. It looks like you tricked them in order to come play for the humans and they don't like being tricked."

"Did I like humans? Before?"

He thought about it. "Don't think you had an opinion on them one way or the other."

That meant I probably hadn't wanted to destroy earth. What a relief. "What was my interest in their war? I know I was planning to stop it."

"You were," he confirmed.

"How?"

Kai shook his head. "If I tell you, you'll only accuse me of lying."

"I won't."

"If you're still anything like Persephone, you will. I know her. Persephone would never believe anything unless she saw it for herself. You'll have to remember. You'll never trust me otherwise. Then we can talk." He stared at me like he wanted to kiss me again, but refrained. "Go inside, Goddess," he said.

There was no point in trying to get anything else out of him. I snatched up my shoes and headed toward the school. I could feel him watching me, so I turned back for one final wave only to see him outside the fence, seemingly conversing with one lone Infernorator.

Damn Hades and all his minions. Especially his son.

7

If you can't beat 'em, poison 'em

ζ '

I was a big ball of crank the next morning, evident by the fact that I was wearing jeans. Considering them the pants of the devil and loaded with body issues, I only stooped to wear jeans when I was in what Hannah called my "little black rain cloud" mood and was unable to summon the energy to pour myself into something better.

Kai was messing with my head. Argh! Not just my head. I hadn't slept all night thinking about him. I couldn't decide if he wanted to screw me or screw me over. Or both. One minute he was kissing me, the next he's all over Bethany, then helping me out by giving me info I desperately need. Where exactly did he stand?

I flung myself into the cafeteria, determined to mow down whomever came between me and my espresso. (Foreign caffeine drinks being a rare perk of my progressive school.)

"That skank," Hannah proclaimed as I joined her, knocking back my espresso in one shot. Much better.

I took a sip of water to clear out my coffee mouth. As I buttered my stack of toast, I craned my neck to see where she was looking. Bethany had her fingers twined in the belt loops of Kai's jeans as they stood in line together. His hand rested on the small of her back. She gave me a smug grin when she saw me staring. I wanted to shove her Bindi back up into her brain. Instead, I turned to Hannah. "She's the poster child."

"Not her," Hannah replied. "Well, her too. But him. Kai. The mimbo. You know, I thought I disliked him when I met him but I'm realizing that my first impression was by far the best. Want me to sic something nasty on him?"

"I'm in a Kai-free zone today. I have bigger things to worry about." I explained to Hannah what I had tried to do last night.

"You're going to get yourself killed," she chided.

"This goddess gig is bound to have side effects." I glared at two sophomores who were attempting to give me "how ya doin'?" nods. "I am so not in the mood."

"Killed unnecessarily," Hannah clarified. "Don't take stupid risks like that. And be nice to the poor boys. They're overwhelmed by your new goddessy hotness."

As if. "Existing in this state is a stupid risk." I complained. "I'm a goddess with blinders on. I need to regain more of my memories." I spied Theo getting in line for breakfast. "I don't even know who to trust. Except you."

"Honestly? You doubt the Rock?" She took a bite of her granola and yogurt.

"I know Theo is my friend," I replied, "and I believe that he saved me. From something. I just don't think he's giving me the full story. He's got some kind of agenda that involves me. He and Kai both. I wish they'd pony up and give me the skinny. Actually," I continued after a moment, "Kai is refusing to, saying I have to remember it for myself or I won't believe him."

"Jeez, Sophie, don't say anything that might make me like him. I was getting comfortable with my disapproval." She thought it over a minute. "Maybe there is something we could do. A kind of meditation to try and unblock your mind."

"Like hypnosis? No way. I won't let you tinker around in my head and have me barking like a dog."

"You have insane trust issues. Not hypnosis. I'm not the Great and Powerful Oz."

"What are you chickens clucking about?" Theo asked as he joined us.

"Kai," I said with a covert warning glance at Hannah.

"He's an asshat," Theo concurred with no hesitation, stabbing a forkful of scrambled eggs.

"He's merely toying with Bethany. Kai is all about me." I tried to sound very confident about that fact.

Theo raised an eyebrow. "Tell me you didn't do him."

"D'uh. You know me, ole 'sex as a weapon' Bloom." I smacked the top of his head. "Although Persephone is big on fertilization."

Theo pushed his food away in disgust. "Never ever put that visual in my head again."

"You need to help Sophie remember," Hannah ordered him sternly. "To fully understand what she's dealing with."

"Yeah. What she said," I added.

"If she hadn't kissed Kai, I wouldn't have a gazillion times more work in getting her up to speed," he groused.

"Cry me a river," I snapped. "You should have kept my memories intact in the first place."

"Your brain couldn't have processed them. You'd have been straitjacketed out in some psych ward and no good to anyone."

"Like Cassie might be now," Hannah reminded us.

Theo and I deflated at that reminder.

"Do you have anything that was Sophie's from when she was Persephone?" Hannah asked. "It might twig her memory."

I reached for my water glass.

Theo gave me a hard look then nodded, as if he'd decided something. "I might," he replied.

I'd been expecting him to say "no" and so I startled at his reply. Water sloshed onto my jeans. I grabbed a napkin to dab at it.

"Wet yourself much?" I heard Bethany ask.

I glanced up. Small mercy, Kai wasn't with her to witness this.

"Does Kai know about this little problem of yours?"

Oh good. She would be sure to tell him. I curled my fingers into fists.

Hannah placed a restraining hand on my arm.

Bethany chuckled and kept going.

"Don't worry," Theo assured me, "she'll get what's coming to her eventually. Girls like that always do."

Hannah and I exchanged an incredulous look.

"No, they don't," I said. Theo may have had all kinds of god knowledge, but he was incredibly naive about the reality of girl politics.

"Whatever," he replied. "Meet me at the front door at noon. Dress warmly. Hannah, you can't come." He stood abruptly and left.

I looked at Hannah, utterly baffled. "I have no clue."

"Me neither," she echoed. "Am I going to be left out of stuff now? The mere mortal as you two very important deities do your high and mighty god stuff?"

"Yes. You'll also need to cover my homework and fetch and carry." I snapped my fingers. "Another espresso."

Hannah stole my last piece of toast. Which was nothing like getting me an espresso, but that was humans for you. Ingrates, the entire species.

The rest of the morning was uneventful. Classes were dull and even if I'd wanted to talk to Ms. Keeper, she was nowhere to be found.

I was en route to meet Theo, having added a warm fleece jacket to my emotional denim armor, when Veronica stopped me. By "stop" I mean she shoved me into a wall and demanded, "Where is she?" Her ponytail bobbed furiously from the force of the shove.

"Who?"

"Bethany. I know you locked her in that bathroom after the dance. What did you do with her now?"

"I'm flattered you think me so capable of making people disappear."

"Don't mess with me, bitch. I'm not kidding around." She grabbed my shirtfront. "Where. Is. She?"

I pushed myself loose. "I have no idea. Why would I want to do anything to her today?"

"Because of Kai. Obviously."

"Missing the connection here."

Veronica shot me a look of disbelief. "Bethany and Kai? Seeing each other?"

Seeing each other? I tried not to let my shock and disgust show.

"You blatantly have the hots for him, not like he'd ever give you the time of day."

He might not give me the time of day but he definitely had no problem sucking face. I kept that little tidbit to myself, though.

"You're also crazy where Bethany is concerned," Veronica went on.

"People in glass houses, Veronica," I cautioned.

"Huh?"

"I saw you desperately trying to get Kai to notice you yesterday. What's it like always being in Bethany's shadow? Being second best. Must suck."

Veronica gaped at me, speechless. I'd never dared to speak to her that way before. But really, on my list of clear and present dangers, she was now on par with dandruff.

"Far as I'm concerned about Bethany, it's good riddance. I'm only sorry I wasn't the one to do it." I stalked off. Always leave on a high note and, for once, I actually had.

Until I took three steps and realized if I hadn't done anything to Bethany, maybe Ms. Keeper had. Maybe this had nothing to do with me and she was just your run-of-the-mill psychopath, preying on kids.

I'm not sure how comforting that thought was, but at least it wasn't personal.

I grabbed Theo's arm and hustled him out the front door. "You're never going to believe this."

I described my encounter with Veronica and explained my theory about Ms. Keeper being a serial killer.

"If that's the case," he said, "don't go anywhere alone with her."

"Theo! We still need to stop her."

"Why us? Call the police."

"Who are they going to believe? Me and my probational Bethany-hating history or a kindly member of our school's staff? No. It's up to us."

"Whatever. First there's somewhere I want to take you." He swung around the side of the school.

"Where? There's nothing out this way except the track."

"And the creek."

True. The creek was pretty small, even for a creek, but it babbled and flowed prettily. Occasionally, on hot days, students stomped through it to cool down, but generally it was deserted. Not deep enough to swim in. Or dangerous enough to drown in.

He stopped at the bank and pulled two small silver bracelets from his jacket pocket.

"What are those?" I asked. "And don't just say 'bracelets.'"

"These puppies will orient us back to the school when it's time to leave."

"Leave from where?"

"Hades," he replied.

"Are you insane? Why?"

"I want to show you something that I think could help recover your memory."

"Breaking and entering? In the Underworld?"

"And theft," Theo added cheerfully.

"No way. I'm following the de-clutter approach to life," I babbled. "Less is more."

"It's just because you don't remember you want this. Trust me. You do."

"No," I hastily protested. "Unless you want me dead, in which case, no freaking way."

"You're not going to die. No one will even know you're there. We're going to sneak in."

"You can't sneak in."

"Why not?" Theo refuted. "Suddenly you're the big expert? People do it all the time."

"Name three," I demanded.

"Hercules, Psyche, and Orpheus. And me."

"Name ten."

He shot me an exasperated look. "We'll be fine."

"And by fine you mean 'dead'? Hades wants to kill me. Generally, you don't make it easy for the homicidal lunatic by going to the place where they are lord and master."

"You have to go. There's something you need to retrieve. It was a gift from your mother, and should be in your possession again."

"I don't care," I lied. "Her parenting leaves a lot to be

desired anyway." I tried to keep my voice steady as I said, "Not like she's bothered to come back for me."

"No one knows where she is. I'm sure she'd come if she could. Which is why you need this. It's all you have left of her."

Damn him. I gave a tense nod.

"Relax."

"How can I relax? You want me to go to Hell."

"No, really," he said. "You need to relax. This is going to hurt." Theo slid one bracelet onto his wrist and the other onto mine. It had a reassuring solidity to it. He grabbed my hand and pulled us into the water.

I screamed as the bracelet twisted into my skin with what felt like a thousand tiny razor-sharp bites. Then something icy cold filled my body. It swirled and expanded within me. I couldn't even catch a breath. This is it, I thought dully, I'm going to die.

Instead, the world shifted and I found myself on a grassless bank, staring at a gigantic river. Which didn't rule out the being dead part, but did make it more watery than I'd anticipated. The sky above was dark but not like a picturesque inky night. More like every bit of light had been sucked out of it.

"Welcome to the Styx," Theo commented dryly. "Our creek is a gateway to the Underworld, if you know how to get through."

I was not amused. I couldn't stop staring at this river which swirled in a corrosive blend of dark oranges and reds. "It looks like the stuff that melted Two-Face," I whispered.

"That was a soothing facial. Trust me. You don't want any part of it to touch you. Also, don't eat anything. Don't drink anything. Unless you want to be stuck here forever. Got it?"

"Got it. How can we even be here?" I asked, incredulous.

I could hear the smile in Theo's voice as I stared, transfixed, at the River Styx. "Magic."

"Like a transporter spell?" I took a couple of steps closer to the water, almost compelled by its sinister beauty.

"No. The creek is a gateway for appropriate people."

"'Appropriate' meaning?"

"Dead," he replied.

I narrowed my eyes and turned to him for the first time since we'd arrived. "Holy cow."

"Yeah. We both look a little different."

Different meaning gray and deceased. "I'm not breathing."

"Perk of being dead?" He patted my arm. "No need. It's part of the 'death up close and personal' experience."

"Tell me this is reversible."

"The water activated the bracelets. Soon as we go back, they deactivate. In theory."

"Theo!"

"Kidding. You have to be dead to cross the river. So we're in a simulated non-living state. Right now, you're a run-of-the-mill, checked out cadaver. Should work enough to get us where we need to go."

"Which is where?"

"The Palace. It was the last place you lived and where

Hades kept this pendant he took from you. You need it back. Might help you remember. Alrighty. Get on."

I glanced at where he was motioning and shook my head violently. "Absolutely, positively not."

Floating before me was a massive raft. On it, a skinny, hunched old man, clad in a black robe, held a large paddling pole. His head was bowed. As the raft bumped gently against the shore, he raised his head. Whoops. Not a man. It was a demon, his ageless, soulless black eyes set in a leathery face with sharply pointed features and a smile like icicles. The big, pointy, dirty kind.

He stretched his back and I realized that he also had black wings folded along his shoulder blades. Judging by their collapsed size, they would be enormous if extended.

"I'm good," I protested again as my treacherous feet headed toward the raft. "What the … ?"

"No choice, Magoo. Dead people have to cross. Don't draw attention to us."

"I don't trust that thing's boat safety skills."

"It's Charon. The ferryman. Been doing this for millennia." Theo jumped aboard the raft.

Charon looked directly at me and I swore that he could see right through to my heart, which would have totally been racing had it actually been beating.

I meekly shuffled into the middle of the raft, careful to avoid his eyes.

"Easy peasy," Theo enthused as we were bumped and jostled from all sides.

Carefully I raised my eyes to see that the raft was

packed with people of all shapes, ages, and sizes. "They're all dead, aren't they?" I asked Theo, glumly.

"Great, isn't it?" He turned to a stocky Japanese man next to him with a bullet wound visible through his head. "Bad business deal?"

"Yes," the man grunted in broken English, "my marriage."

"Who did you get these crackpot bracelets from, anyway?" I whispered.

He shrugged. "I still have my resources. I am a very well loved Titan."

"Wouldn't the correct form be 'was a very well loved Titan' since your boney human butt bears zero resemblance to anything titanic at the moment?"

"You think busting my chops is in your best interests right now?" he chided.

Fine. I had bigger things to occupy me. Like terror. This wasn't the smoothest ride. Apparently being dead didn't earn you an easy passage. I sat paralyzed in the middle of the raft as the devil water sprayed and frothed around us.

On the plus side, the raft got a bit emptier as the occasional dead person got taken out by the River Styx.

I have no idea how long we were on the raft but it felt like forever before it stopped.

"Finally," I exclaimed, ready to bound to shore.

Theo stopped me with a shake of his head. "Not here. This is Tartarus. For the evil doers. Going to be a lot of massive regret in about thirty seconds.

I was surprised when about half the figures on our

raft disembarked. They'd seemed like such nice dead people. I craned my neck to take in the fence of bronze that stretched high and wide into infinity. "Doesn't seem so bad."

Then the cries started. It was the sound of a million souls damned into a frozen eternity. I flashed back to that place of dark terror I'd seen the night I kissed Kai. Tartarus. For some reason, I'd been behind that fence before.

The sounds overwhelmed me with despair. I sat down hard on the raft. All I wanted was to lay down and die. I started to fall back but before I could get anywhere, Theo grasped my arm, digging his fingers into it painfully. "Leave me alone," I moaned.

"Fight it. Dead people have no emotions. If you cave, you'll unbind to your true form and we'll be killed. Come on," he urged. "Neutralize the despair. Think of things you like. Chocolate, sarcasm, Hannah …"

I didn't care. The raft pushed off again with a bump.

"Remember that time Bethany let you leave the bathroom with your skirt tucked into your underwear? Or when she loaned you her pen that leaked and you were covered in ink just in time for class photos?"

"This is your way of cheering me up?" Luckily, the farther away we got from Tartarus, the better I felt. "That was horrible."

"Don't worry. Our next stop will amaze."

He was right. We were finally able to disembark at the foot of Hades' palace, built entirely of dark green, marbled stone. While nothing bloomed in its gardens, the grounds were filled with statues and the bright moonlight cast a silvery glow over everything.

We wandered up a long stoney path toward the main doors, past a still pool, obsidian black, ringed with silver twisted trees. It was oddly calming. I remembered it as The Pool of Lethe. Hades had spirits drink from it when they had trouble accepting their new reality.

We rounded a corner and hit a crowded area. I tried not to gape. This was the ultimate in people watching. I scooted out of the way of a pair of old biddies, tottering on impossibly high heels, their hair teased and lips hideously overblown.

"Fashion victims," Theo whispered. "Death by collagen injection."

I muffled a laugh as we passed under a stone archway and approached a pair of ornately carved iron doors decorated with scenes of gods in battle.

"The war of the Titans," Theo explained. He motioned to one panel which showed a god receiving a helmet from a Cyclops. "Hades getting the Cap of Invisibility. Droned on about that stupid hat for eons. Big deal. It's not like it fit 'ole One Eye."

Theo gazed at the door a moment longer, a sad look on his face. I wondered if he was depicted on a panel. I would have asked him but he pivoted sharply and strode off.

I lingered, reaching out a finger to trace a detail. I could have examined the doors for hours. They were stunning and intricately crafted. But Theo had already gone inside, so I reluctantly tore my gaze away and hurried after him.

I found myself in a cavernous room. The walls were hewn from the same large blocks of green stone as outside. It was as vast as a football field and empty save for a large throne set on a base halfway across. Theo stood beside the throne, waiting for me.

I made my way across the slick, jet-black floor warily. The throne seemed to rise from the ground like an island from the sea. Cut from one giant block of obsidian, it stood thirty feet tall. Even getting to the foot of the throne from its base took about ten tremendous stairs. How large were these gods?

"Here's the Cliff notes," Theo began. "You know that Hades is Lord of the Underworld. He's not the Christian interpretation of Satan. Not pure evil. Totally power-mad and arrogant, though, like his brothers. Hades is obsessed with gaining a bigger share than he got. And he's raised junior to be the same."

Some things were coming back to me. "Yeah. And Kai was getting tired of waiting for the throne. Hades always put him off, going on about how great Hades himself was, and how disappointing Kai was. Kai was going to do something about it."

"Just Kai?" Theo countered.

I couldn't answer him so I climbed the stairs at the base to examine the throne.

Kai and I stood on the base, having been summoned by Hades. The Lord of the Underworld lounged lazily on his throne, attended by an entourage of nymphs. In one fist he grasped a wineskin from which he drank greedily. His face, still handsome, showed the toll of his excessive pleasure taking.

"My son," he boomed to his various sycophants. "Your next ruler of Hades." He sneered. "A whelp enthralled by a slut of Zeus."

I hated him. How could my father and mother have left me here? Why hadn't they taken Kai and me away back up to Olympus?

"Better enthralled by a goddess then pawing desperately at any half-female, willing or not," Kai shot back.

"I rue the day I sired you," Hades glowered. He shifted, revealing a brilliant round sapphire set into the centre of the throne.

"Not more than I," Kai retorted.

I snapped my head up. The gemstone was still there. I clambered up onto the seat.

The sapphire called to me. "Daughter of Demeter, born of Zeus," I murmured. "My mom gave me this when I was born …"

"… And Hades took it away when he kidnapped you," Theo finished.

I nodded. "No one besides than me can handle it, so Hades made me set it into the throne for him, just to rub it in. Then he cast some spell on the stone so that if anyone tried to steal it, he'd know."

I shot a cocky grin at Theo. "Luckily, I figured that one out ages ago. He would have noticed if I kept it, but he couldn't prevent me from holding it." I was thrilled at how much was rushing back to me. "Hat tip to you, Theo, for bringing me back to this baby."

"Pleasure's all mine," Theo replied.

I rubbed my hands together to warm them. The trick was to place my palm over the entire stone, binding the pendant to my skin. I sighed in delight as I felt it adhere. Then bit by painfully slow bit, I pulled my hand back, drawing the sapphire with it. It pulsed at my touch.

Finally, the pendant popped free. I held it up to the light. Only a couple inches in diameter and about the size of a small egg, it was finely etched. A tiny silver loop at the top could be used to thread a chain.

One etching showed a thunderbolt, the other a sheaf of wheat. The symbols of my two parents. I clasped it tightly in my palm. For not knowing it existed ten minutes ago, I was incredibly relieved to have the gem back in my possession.

"You really have to stop touching my things."

The menace underneath that silky tone sent shivers down my spine. Hades. He may have been massive at twenty feet tall, but the past sixteen years hadn't done him any favors. He appeared even more bloated and red-faced. His once jet black hair was now shot through with a lot of white. Even so, he exuded an enormous amount of charisma. There was something incredibly compelling about the god, despite his scariness. Probably where his son got it.

I straightened my shoulders, my head held high, trying not to feel like an ant before an elephant. "How did you know I was here?"

"As if I wouldn't know what was going on in my realm? The second you removed the gem, you triggered an alarm."

Theo shot me an "I thought you knew what you were doing" look.

Hades smiled. Not kindly. "Hello, Prometheus."

"Wasn't sure you'd recognize me," Theo said.

"Who else would accompany our Persephone? But don't blame her. The moment I discovered she'd been murdered, I changed the spell on the stone." He sighed as if weary. "I'm not surprised. She was too irritating to truly be dead."

"Now what, Hades?" Theo sounded bored. "Torture? Fiery death?"

I elbowed him. Why give Hades ideas?

"Wine."

Not the answer I'd been expecting.

Hades plucked me off his throne and ushered us around to the back of it. I thought his touch would be scaly, cold, and evil. Not so. His meaty fingers were surprisingly smooth and warm. I guess he didn't do a lot of manual labor. He placed his hands on the base, splayed his fingers and pushed.

I gasped as a huge block of stone swung open to reveal a door in the base.

Hades manhandled us through.

I felt a moment of fear as the door silently swung closed again, blocking us in, but curiosity got the better of me.

As black as the outside of the base had been, the inside

radiated a warm gold. Because it was gold. I whistled. A hallway led off the room. I could see far enough into it to know that it sloped steeply. It must have led under the floor of the throne room.

I glanced up at the ceiling to see if it was gold as well—which it was—but was distracted by a black iron chandelier. I knew that lighting fixture. "Oh!" I inhaled sharply. "That light. I stared at it … after …" A flood of images assaulted me, none of them pleasant. I grasped my sides reliving the agony of my murder once again.

"It's just a memory," Theo soothed. "It can't hurt you."

"Such a good day, your death. We could always reenact it." Hades sounded amused with himself.

I'd been paralyzed from a dart in my side. I slumped to the floor, unable to hold up my own weight. I tried to scream, but my voice didn't work. Someone laughed. I tried to see who, but couldn't.

"This is where you found me?" Theo nodded in response.

"Any thoughts on how you got here?" Hades spoke in a tone of utter disinterest. I couldn't tell if he really wanted to know or was bluffing.

Either way, I wasn't going to give him the satisfaction.

"Going to murder me outright now?" I accused. "You hid behind your Cap of Invisibility the first time."

Hades frowned. "If I'd killed you, my face would have been the last thing you'd seen." His expression changed to that of kindly host. "You look pale. Come. Sit." He led us to an enormous pile of throw cushions on the ground, each one of which was sofa-sized for Theo and me.

I surreptitiously slid the pendant into the pocket of my fleece jacket. I was hoping for out of sight, out of mind as far as Hades was concerned.

He saw me and smiled, amused. "You can hold on to your trinket." The "for now" was implied.

We'd see about that. This gem was coming with me, no matter what.

Hades clapped his hands.

A winged baby emerged from the hallway, hovering in mid-air, a tray with two small and one much larger wine goblet in his hands. No cutie pie, him. He was more like "Children of the Corn" creepified by a zillion. I began shivering with terror. Theo stroked my back to keep me calm.

"You don't remember Thanatos? Death?" asked Hades.

I gasped at the reveal of the baby's name.

"The false one hurts my feelings," Thanatos said dryly, in a surprisingly low voice. "Wine?"

I recalled Theo's warnings and shook my head. I didn't trust my voice to speak.

"No? Shame. Such a good vintage." Hades drank deeply from his own glass. "Something to eat, then?"

I looked between Hades, Lord of the Underworld, lounging in front of me with his booze, and the floating death baby with the rumbly voice and felt hysterical laughter bubble up inside me. One way or another I was going to be killed yet again in this place.

"Sure," I tossed out, numb. "Pomegranates."

"Soph," Theo warned.

"What?" I laughed. "I really think fruit is the least of our worries right now, Theo."

"I give you my word no harm will come to you from the food or drink," Hades said. "There are so many other ways to destroy you."

"Still. We're good," Theo reiterated, as a bearded young man, who happened to be both naked and have wings spouting from his head arrived. Guess they were just for show, as he was planted firmly on the ground. He presented me with a large silver bowl of pomegranate seeds.

"It is my pleasure to serve you. Your love of this fruit is legendary." Naked guy sounded like he was a two-pack-a-day man. I recalled he was Hypnos, a.k.a. Sleep. The twin to Death. I guess "twin" had a lot more leeway in Greek than in English.

I averted my eyes from Hypnos' unattractive nudity.

"We're not going to eat or drink," Theo said. "So just get on with whatever you're planning on doing to us." Ten points for Theo's cockiness but minus a million for trying to get us killed a second sooner than we had to be.

Hades shrugged. "Your choice." He tossed back a handful of seeds. Suddenly he turned a violent shade of purple and clutched at his throat, coughing.

"My Lord!" Hypnos and Thanatos flew to his side.

Theo grabbed my hand and yanked me to my feet as Hypnos stared down at his bowl in horror. "The goddess. She called for the seeds."

"You've poisoned Hades!" Baby roared. "And now you will die!"

The ginormous God of the Underworld was potentially dying and it looked like I'd encouraged him to snarf the poison. Throw in my motive for wanting revenge for attempted murder, and saying "I didn't do it" probably wasn't going to cut it with his evil minions.

Time to blow this joint, and fast.

8
It takes two to tangle
η′

We ran for our lives. Instinct and adrenaline fueled me. Sometimes Theo was in the lead, sometimes I was. But we both seemed to have the same destination.

Many twists and turns down the hallway under the throne room and we burst out through a door onto the grounds of the palace, cutting off Hypnos' and Thanatos' pursuit and buying us a few critical seconds.

The earth shook violently under our feet as we fled. Theo grabbed my hand and we continued at breakneck speed. About a hundred feet ahead of us was a large, ornate fountain. "Our way out!" he yelled, as we tried not to be upended by the rolling ground.

Only eighty feet to the fountain when a burst of flame hit my sleeve.

"Theo!"

"Move!" he ordered.

I bashed at my flaming arm as best I could while sprinting. The sky above us had filled with Pyrosim. Fire rained down on us, fast and furious. I could feel it sparking in my hair.

Thirty feet to the fountain. "Dive!" Theo shouted,

pulling on my hand. "But don't look back!" He pulled me down in an action hero roll.

As we hit the ground, I was aware of a giant shadow soaring over me, landing somewhere at my back.

Before I could figure out what it was, the ground in front of me burst into flame from a direct hit from above. With no way to switch direction, momentum carried me right through it. Only the fact that I was still rolling and therefore smothering the fire saved me from becoming a one girl tiki torch.

Theo violently yanked me to my feet milliseconds later. I risked a look over my shoulder and screamed involuntarily.

On our heels was Cerberus, the hound of hell. He had bounded over us and now turned back in our direction for the hunt. As tall as he was wide, he was a canine killing machine. *Hel-lo*, Cujo.

Each of his three heads displayed massive fangs as they snarled and barked at us. His tail was scaly and spiked like that of a dragon and his massive paws ended in sharp claws. Every inch of the beast promised death.

"Told you not to look," Theo yelled.

For a girl who could barely run around the track, I may have broken some Olympic records. I could feel Cerberus' hot breath getting closer. I braced myself for the feel of his jaws ripping into me and crunching me to bits. By this point, I'd totally forgotten about the fire.

One of Cerberus' heads snatched the back of my jacket. I knew this was the end. But by some fluke of luck, the ground quaked so violently that I was flung from his grasp just long enough for Theo to tumble us into the water in the fountain, through the gateway, and back to the school.

We were safe.

We were also filthy, ragged, and scorched. None of which mattered, because when I saw blue sky above my head, I felt reborn.

Also wet, because we were laying in the creek. My jeans had shrunk in the cold water. Which was funny since they should have expanded from the two tons of creek it felt like they'd absorbed. "I know we should get up but—" I was cut off by the creek bed bucking beneath me.

"The Underworld rages," Theo said as we crawled onto the shore to wait out the earthquake. Normally I would have found this terrifying but after our little adventure, a minor natural disaster was a step in the right direction.

Cerberus' heads popped through, spraying water as they lashed out at me. Oh. Thing wanting me dead. Go back one step.

His front half emerged from the creek.

Without thinking, a ribbon of light snaked out of my left hand and, with one whipping motion, hefted a boulder from the creek bed at him. It cracked him hard enough to knock him back into Hades.

Cerberus disappeared and the rumbling stopped.

Finally, all was quiet.

I got to my feet. "Nice stealth moves there, buddy. Real safe. Remind me not to travel with you again any time soon."

"We got the pendant, we're alive. Pretty successful trip if you ask me." Theo looked at me hopefully. "Did retrieving it trigger your goddess memories?"

I shook my head. "No. Sorry."

"I had hoped …" He frowned. "You always wore the sapphire. I thought if you had it back, it would help key you in to your Persephone self."

"I do feel better for having it," I assured him. "It just didn't help me remember anything. Is there anything else it does?"

Theo shrugged. "Only you would know that."

"Even if the sapphire is just a pendant with no special powers, my mom gave it to me and for me, that makes it priceless. Plus, Hades all busy being poisoned means he forgot to take it away from me. Of course, there is still the major downside that *we're* the ones framed for it." I gasped. "Is Hades dead? Are we going to be accused of murdering him?" Oh, that would be bad.

Theo shook his head. "I've never heard of anything that could actually kill the old bastard. He's down, but probably not out."

And yet, that wasn't much of a relief. "How could anyone know we'd be there to take the blame? Or was it just an unlucky coincidence?"

"I didn't tell anyone we were going." Theo was grim. "But unless we figure out who was behind it, we'll never be able to clear our names. You asking for the stupid seeds combined with us not eating them after Hades promised us immunity? We look guilty. All of the Underworld will be gunning for us. Worse than before."

I snapped my fingers. "Cassie! If she foresaw my transformation back to Persephone, what else could she know about? The Oracle had visions, right? What if Cassie saw the deception down in Hades? She might know who poisoned us. And that info might be the difference between life and death. Ours."

"It makes finding her even more important," Theo agreed. "So we hit up Keeper's office. Get something to lead us to either Cassie or Keeper herself."

"I thought this ground was protected," I said, as we made our way back across the grass. "How did Cerberus get through?"

"We had the gateway open. Your boulder trick must have shut it down."

"What's to prevent our enemies from coming through the gateway again?"

"Still warded. They can't open it so long as they intend to harm us. Us giving them an opening? Different story."

"Let's not do that anymore, then," I muttered, as we continued on our weary way. I got up the courage to ask what I'd been wondering about for a while now. I turned bleak eyes on him. "What did I look like? When I was ... attacked."

"You don't want to know."

"I do."

Theo sighed. "Whatever they'd used to stab you had been enchanted, because the wounds bled out very slowly. For maximum pain. It was horrible. You couldn't move. Just stared blankly up at the chandelier as your life force drained out of you. I barely transferred you out of your body in time."

I shuddered, feeling that lethal limbo all over again. The moment was all too clear. But I wouldn't let it swallow me. Again. "I'm going to figure out who did it and kill them, Theo."

We came into view of the school. It appeared fine. No visible damage. Inside, everything was calm. Too calm.

"Where is everyone?" I wondered.

"Yeah. You'd think there'd be a few hissy fits after the quake," Theo agreed.

"Theo, Sophie," Principal Doucette loomed up before us as he stepped out from the cafeteria. "Do I even want to know what you've been up to?"

"The earthquake," I said. "Didn't you feel it?"

He took a good look at us and frowned. "No. Where were you?"

"Out by the creek," Theo replied.

Principal Doucette shook his head. "We felt nothing here. Get changed and dry, then get yourselves to Nurse Hamata's office. Then Sophie, Ms. Keeper wants to see you. Something about an assignment you didn't turn in." He focused on Theo. "And you have a class to get to."

"That truth exercise," I said to Theo as we headed for the nurse's office after a quick detour to change into dry clothes. I never wanted to see those jeans again.

I threaded the pendant on a silver chain and hung it around my neck, hiding the priceless sapphire under my shirt. I felt more confident with it on and I knew that I'd never remove it while alive again.

"You have to come with me to see Ms. Keeper," I instructed Theo. "No way am I letting a potential psychopath get me alone."

The school nurse, a plump Japanese woman with a constantly bright smile, patched us up in no time. "Nurse Hamata," I asked, "is Cassie all right? Did she go home?"

"Who?"

"Cassandra Jones."

"The ginger," Theo added helpfully.

Nurse Hamata was blank. "Is she new?"

Theo and I exchanged worried looks. "No, ma'am."

Nurse Hamata blinked. "I can't help you. I don't know this student." She patted my arm cheerfully. "Off you two go. All better."

Theo waited until we were out in the hallway to speak. "That was beyond weird."

"Definitely," I agreed. "How could she forget Cassie? Was she hypnotized or something?"

"Pretty powerful something."

A Hannah squeal pierced my ears. "Ohmigod, what happened to you guys? You look awful!"

"Theo made me do a little tour of Hades. It got bumpy."

"Whoa. Seriously? Why?"

I showed her the pendant while I filled her in about Theo's hope that it would retrieve my memories.

Hannah considered this. "Did it help?"

"Nope." I decided not to mention the whole Hades poisoning incident. It would just freak her out.

"Sorry, kiddo," she consoled. "You going to be all right? I've gotta hit the library."

"One sec," Theo said, "you remember Cassandra, right?"

"Sure," she replied.

We gave a sigh of relief.

"The Greek Oracle."

"No. The student."

Hannah crinkled her brow. "Is she new?"

I grabbed her shoulders and shook her. "Hannah! Cassie. Went missing? Maybe Kai stole her? You were really worried about her a couple of hours ago?"

She shrugged, clueless.

"We're off to find Ms. Keeper," I said. "Hannah, stay with us."

"I've got this assignment."

"Humor me. I don't want you fading from memory while my back is turned."

"Twenty minutes. Then you follow me into the stacks."

Along the way, we passed Veronica, all flounced up and striding down the hall like a girl on a mission.

"Guess Bethany resurfaced," I called out, since she didn't look like someone who'd literally lost her best friend.

"Who?"

I huffed in frustration. "You've got to be kidding."

"Whatever," she smirked, curling the end of her ponytail around her finger. "I'm off to meet Kai."

"Yeah, and twenty other kids. Class isn't a date, Veronica," Hannah pointed out.

"It is if you do it right." She pushed past us sashaying off down the hallway.

"No Bethany? Ding dong, the witch is gone," Theo cheered. "Champagne anyone?"

I sighed in disappointment. "I can't celebrate. We have to find her."

"'With great power comes great responsibility, Spider-man,'" Theo replied.

"Yeah. I hate that. Three days ago I'd have been thrilled she was gone. Now, I feel all responsible."

"That whole taking care of humanity thing," Hannah pointed out as we made our way to Ms. Keeper's office. "We're your duty."

"Doesn't mean I have to like it."

"It's good for you. Now, who's Bethany?"

This was insane. How could Hannah not remember? "What happened when we were in Hades?"

Theo shook his head, a worried expression on his face. "The only thing I can think of is that someone put a giant memory spell on everyone."

"Keeper, maybe? But why?"

"No pesky questions asked if you can't remember a person is missing?" Theo guessed. "Or two specific ones so far. The Oracle—"

"And Bethany. But she's nothing special. So why her?" I wondered.

Theo shrugged. "Maybe she was just an expendable bystander? I don't know."

"And *we* remember Cassie and Bethany why?"

"My Prometheus knowledge transferred and your Persephone identity has been awakened. Bet Kai remembers, too."

We reached Ms. Keeper's office and I knocked. "Stay with me at all times," I admonished.

"Got it," Hannah said. "She still after you?"

"Probably just one of those balmy serial killers burying kids under the floorboards," Theo said.

"So it's not about Sophie," she replied. "And yet potentially more dangerous to the rest of us."

"Yeah. Pretty much," he agreed.

We entered the counseling room. Other than your run-of-the mill office furniture, affirmative posters, and a couch for students to cry on, it was empty.

"That was anti-climatic," I said.

"Are you stupid, or just insane?" Kai had arrived to the party and was glaring at me like I'd plummeted to new lows in his estimation.

"I didn't do it," I replied, heading toward Theo and Hannah to make my escape.

"No kidding." Kai blocked me. "I meant going there in the first place." He glanced at the chain around my neck. Quickly, he tugged the pendant out.

I slapped his hand away and placed the stone back against my chest.

"You couldn't pull off poisoning a god," he said.

I batted my eyelashes at him sweetly. "You're right. Silly little me would have no clue. But you would."

"Sophie," Theo hissed in warning. "Shut up."

I ignored him. "And here's an interesting fact. Right before Hades choked, I smelled this distinct aroma. Similar to bitter coffee? Funny enough, I smelled the same thing when I was murdered. Who would use an identical poison on both Hades and me? Maybe a guy who hates his dad and flirts with other girls when his girlfriend comes back from the dead?" I shoved Kai out of the way.

"You're not my girlfriend," he replied.

"No kidding. Since I'm breaking up with you on behalf of Persephone. There. Now you're my ex."

Theo shook his head. "Here we go again," he muttered.

Kai stepped in close to me. "You think because you have her powers, you're her?" He laughed, mirthlessly. "You don't have the faintest clue."

"Fact. I don't need my memories back to know how much I dislike you. Some things are just bone deep," I shot back.

"Fact," Kai mimicked, "if I'd murdered you, I'd have stuck around to make sure I did the job properly the first time. Although practice makes perfect."

"You guys are better than cable," Hannah exclaimed, entranced.

"I'm outta here," I announced.

"God, no. Me first, please," Theo begged, trying to get ahead of me in my flight to the door.

Kai got to the door before I could, slammed it shut and leaned against it. "No one is going anywhere until we get a few things straight."

"That would be 'straight' according to your agenda, would it?" asked Theo.

"You really wanna go there, Prometheus, then let's do this. Why don't you tell Persephone—"

"Sophie" I interjected.

"Who summoned her to the gold chamber that day?"

I looked at Theo, confused. "What's he talking about?"

"He's off his head," Theo retorted.

"I heard you," Kai insisted. "You told her to meet you there."

I turned hurt eyes to Theo. I couldn't believe it.

"It wasn't me," Theo vowed. "Not the attack."

"Why were you the one who found me? Don't tell me it was coincidence." I wasn't going to let this go.

Hannah was seated on Ms. Keeper's desk, following the whole exchange, rapt.

Theo stayed mum.

"Tell me," I demanded.

"I was supposed to meet Demeter. I wanted you to see her. But she didn't show and there you were."

That was about the last thing I expected to hear. Kai too, from the stunned look on his face.

"No way," he refuted. "She couldn't have gotten into the Underworld back then. With Hades all freaked that Persephone would be stolen back? He had that place on lockdown. No ally of Zeus' would have been able to enter."

"She was pretty convinced she'd be able to. I figured she had inside help."

"Don't look at me," Kai retorted. "She's the last person I'd have wanted down there."

"Oh, I believe you, bro," Theo replied. "Can't imagine you wanted a face-to-face with Demeter after stealing her kid."

"Could you have been the one helping Demeter?" This

from Hannah. Three pairs of eyes swung my way. "She is your mom."

"I don't know."

"Convenient little amnesia scam you've got going," Kai muttered.

"Aw. You figured it out. One dash of no freaking clue who I am, add stupid guys I can't trust and presto. Super evil scam to take over the world. Gonna need a lair though."

"The kitchen," Hannah suggested cheerfully. "Definitely an evil vibe there."

"Hey!" Theo was still stuck on my "stupid guys" remark. "You can trust me."

Kai snorted.

"Jerk," Theo scoffed. "If you hadn't cocked this all up because you couldn't keep it in your pants, we wouldn't be in this trouble."

"Exactly," I echoed.

Kai turned on me. "Poor little human. Stolen kiss in the moonlight. Pretty exciting for you, huh?"

"I am willing to break all kinds of immortality laws to take this dickhead out," Hannah said to me.

"He's right, Soph," Theo said. "You can't compare. Kai's a real god. Banging everything in sight these past sixteen years. Just like his dad."

Kai swung around with a look of surprise. Theo smirked. "Yeah, even I heard about your exploits. Doing the old man proud, are we?"

"Take it back," Kai said in a low voice.

"Make me," Theo challenged.

In a burst of inhuman speed, Kai grabbed Theo by the neck in a chokehold. "Just one little snap. Humans break so easily. Can't imagine why you'd want to become one."

Theo wedged one hand between his neck and Kai's arm to keep an airway. With the other, he reached down and snapped off the chain holding his wallet to his pants. Immediately it began to glow with a hot white light as it doubled in length.

My eyes widened as Theo whipped the chain around Kai's arm and spun himself free, retracting the chain with a snap. I could smell the burning flesh. Theo took several steps back, faced Kai and wrapped one end of the chain around his fist for a better grip.

"That had to hurt," Hannah whispered.

Kai didn't even look at his burned arm. He narrowed his eyes at the chain and then smiled like he was pleased to see it. Whatever turned his crank.

Theo shot him a cocky grin. "Just because I'm human doesn't make me stupid." He snapped the chain at Kai. "Come closer if you want, but she's a nasty bit of business. Forged by order of Zeus himself. The master at inflicting pain."

"It's the chain that was used to bind him to the rock," Hannah gasped.

"Quit it. Both of—" I tried to interject but had to grab Hannah and scramble out of the way as Kai blasted Theo with a black light that somehow seemed to come to a point. Like a really nasty sword that wouldn't just play nice and pierce you to death. The light seemed to have depth and a very creepy, well, wriggliness to it.

Theo deflected it with the chain like it was a solid object and Kai's light struck Ms. Keeper's desk.

The spot in which Hannah had been seated seconds ago was instantly incinerated into a pile of smoking ash.

It looked toxic. I gingerly reached out a toe to poke at it—

"Sophie!" Theo snapped.

Guess it was toxic. I pulled my foot back.

"He can't do that!" Hannah sputtered, swiveling her head between the Hazmat waste on the floor and the boys fighting with impossible weapons.

"Which one?" I asked.

"Either!"

Apparently, this had all just been foreplay for the boys because that's when their fight began in earnest. Hannah and I were trapped across the room from the door, taking refuge behind a filing cabinet. Until Theo split it in two with his chain like slicing a giant pat of butter.

We jumped behind the sofa. That didn't last long either as Theo jumped on it for a better angle to attack Kai and Kai blasted him. Theo survived. The sofa didn't.

As the debris flew, Hannah and I sprinted to our last refuge; the bookcase. We frantically pulled it far enough away from the wall so that we could squeeze ourselves in behind it.

"Can't you do anything?" Hannah asked.

"Oh, yeah! I can."

Hannah glared at me.

"Don't be all huffy. I'm still getting used to it." I

stepped out from behind the bookcase, taking care to avoid all ash piles.

It was no holds barred between Theo and Kai. Both were bleeding, not from hits but from blasted furniture fallout.

For a human, Theo was amazing. But Kai was a blur, his speed and strength giving him the edge. He was a fighting machine, seemingly completely relaxed and yet not missing a single step. The way his eyes were glinting made me think he was getting off on this.

I kept from dwelling on how hot he was by reminding myself that the last thing Kai needed was another groupie. I hated him. My ex. I'd never had an ex but I was glad it was him because—

Kai spun and I tilted my head to get a better look at his very fine butt.

"Sophie!" Hannah nudged me sharply with an elbow.

"Right." I had a job to do. Not that that kept me from looking twice.

I aimed one hand at each of the guys and shot out ribbons of light to wrap around their ankles. I lifted them up and dangled them in mid-air. That stopped them.

"Light really shouldn't behave like that," Hannah said.

"I know, right?" It was way cool. Back to the boys. "Now that I have your attention," I began.

Theo apparently didn't care that he was hanging upside down. He snapped his chain at Kai. I panicked and managed to drop my hold on Kai, sending him crashing to the ground.

Theo's chain missed him entirely and smashed into a window. Oddly, no glass rained down on us.

"That was unexpected." I lowered Theo to the ground and pointed to the row of three windows. In the centre one, where there should have been a gaping hole to the outside, was a perfect square of blue light.

I put my hand up to it.

Kai snatched me back before I made contact. "Do you touch hot stoves, too?"

"It's a window frame," I said.

"That could have some kind of trigger around it. You're lucky your hand wasn't cut off. Or worse."

"He's right," Theo agreed. "That was fairly daft." Holding tight to one end, Theo flung his chain toward the square of blue.

We all watched as Theo's chain crashed and rebounded off an invisible barrier right at the window frame.

For a second, nothing more happened, then suddenly there was a loud WHUMP noise and a flurry of motion as a bevy of arrows shot across from right side of the frame to embed themselves in the left.

I waited for Kai to gloat.

"Too easy," he said.

"Like your standards, dating Bethany?" I murmured.

"Jealous, are we?"

Please. As. If. He and I were *so* ancient history. "Whatever."

Theo peered at the window frame. "It's warded," he said.

I groaned. "Great. We'll never get through."

Kai slanted a look my way. "Why not?"

"Intention to harm? We'll never bypass it."

"You really forgot everything, didn't you?"

I crossed my arms, disliking his tone. "Enlighten me."

Kai crossed *his* arms and shot me a "why should I?" look.

I re-crossed my arms right back at him and shot him a "because you need me" smile.

"Just tell us already," Hannah said.

I got the feeling that our fight was not over, just kind of put on hold. But Kai did explain.

"There are different types of wards. Some, like the one Theo has at Hope Park, are based on intention to harm."

"Figured that out, did you?" Theo muttered.

Kai shot him a cool look. "Wasn't too hard after Sophie nearly killed herself going after a Pyrosim."

I squirmed under Theo's stare. "I may have forgotten to fill you in about that."

Theo swung his gaze back to Kai. "Convenient of you to happen to be there."

"Doing my part to keep Sophie safe."

Theo didn't bother to respond to that whopper.

I didn't either.

Kai continued. "Some wards are like a closed door. The person warding it doesn't really expect anyone to follow so they don't deadbolt it. Just close it. Maybe booby-trap it. But if you know how to open it and avoid the trap? Instant access."

"She'd hidden the passageway behind the window and

figured anyone who managed to find it would be killed by the arrows," Hannah said.

Kai inclined his head. "Exactly."

"So how do we get inside?"

"Give me a minute," Theo muttered, examining the frame.

Hannah looked around at the mess that had been made of the room. "What happens if we touch the ash?"

Kai glanced down at a pile. "Nothing, now that it's cooled off."

Hannah nodded. "Back in a sec." She left, shutting the office door behind her.

With Theo focused on the ward, that left Kai and me staring at each other. A contest of wills. As I gazed into his fathomless eyes, it occurred to me that this was one staring contest I wasn't going to win. "Guess you didn't take that long to get over me," I said, hoping for a sneak blink attack.

It worked. Ha ha. "All those other females to plug," he replied. I couldn't tell if he was being sarcastic or not.

"So much for 'you're my universe,'" I muttered, then caught myself, startled at the memory.

"You were." He sounded equally startled.

An openly hostile fight I could deal with this. Whatever this was, I couldn't. Because however Kai felt about me, it was too loaded a discussion to get into right now. Or was the problem what he didn't feel about me, Sophie, but *had* felt about me, Persephone? How was a girl supposed to compete with herself?

Time for a new topic of conversation. "I'm sorry about your dad. Even though he's a son-of-a-bitch."

Kai laughed; a bitter sound. "Remember that much, do you?"

"One thing I can't remember. Did we ever go to Olympus? Or were we always in Hades?"

"We couldn't go to Olympus. I wouldn't have been safe there."

"But I was safe in the Underworld?"

"Long as I was around, you were."

"Where'd you go, then? When I was attacked." I tried for nonchalant.

I failed.

"Hades had sent me on an errand." He seemed kind of evasive.

"Doing what?"

Kai avoided my eyes. "Stealing Zeus' thunderbolt."

Theo turned with raised eyebrows at that. I motioned for him to focus back on the window frame.

"Bold move there, son," I told Kai.

He glanced at me, surprised. "You're not mad?"

"Why would I be mad?"

"He is your dad."

"Of whom I have very little memory. Don't forget, he sent a Gold Crusher to take me out. Not so much on the family fuzzies."

Hannah returned with cheap plastic gloves, a few pairs of tweezers, and a wad of sealable plastic bags.

I raised an eyebrow. "Holy CSI, Batman."

Hannah handed me the gloves. "Anything that seems

like a promising clue to explain the ward? Or anything else out of the ordinary? Use the tweezers to pick it up. Then bag it. Even slivers. I can put them under the microscope later."

She held one pair of tweezers to Kai who ignored it until Hannah was forced to give it to me, instead. "Ever seen an Inland Taipan snake?" she asked him, threateningly.

"You do get that I'm immortal, right?" Kai retorted.

"Immortal is not the same thing as unkillable," she replied sweetly.

Theo chuckled.

I combed gingerly through the ash for a plausible clue. "How'd you do it?" I asked. "Steal the thunderbolt."

Kai gave me a rueful smile. "I didn't. We'd heard that Zeus was headed to see Poseidon for a secret meeting. I was supposed to steal it from him there. But it was an ambush."

"You weren't even in Hades when I was attacked." My relief was overwhelming.

"Yeah, he was," Theo chimed in, arching his back to stretch it out. "I saw him minutes before I found you."

My stomach dropped. I was never going to get to the truth of the matter.

"I had just gotten back," Kai said defensively. "And Pers—Sophie, was supposed to be on earth."

"Why's that?" Theo mused.

"None of your business," Kai replied.

"It's *my* business," I said, bagging what appeared to be a broken fingernail.

"Yup. And when you remember it, you'll know."

"You're particularly infuriating, you know that?"

Anything else I was going to say was cut short by Hannah's excited squeal. "Check it out," she enthused. She held up an indigo iridescent scale about three inches in diameter. "Wonder what it's from? Theo?" She noted his pale look. "You're not scared of reptiles are you?"

"I am when they're that."

"Dragon," Kai said grimly. "One's come to Hope Park."

9
A dead minion tells no tales
θ′

"Dragon? Tell me that means 'fluffy kitten' in Greek."
Kai shot me a look of disgust.

"So that's what's taken Cassie and Bethany?"

"Maybe." Theo didn't sound certain.

I stomped my foot and pointed at the blue light inside the empty window frame. "Cassie and Bethany could be in there right now. In danger."

"That's awful," Hannah said. "Who are they?"

I growled in annoyance. "How do we fix this?" I hated what had happened to them.

"First find out exactly what Ms. Keeper is," Theo said.

"Apparently, she's a dragon," Hannah replied with shining eyes.

"Or she has a dragon," Theo countered.

Hannah shook her head. "Even if this dragon is akin to a Komodo and trainable, there should have been other evidence of its presence."

"You know this from your extensive experience with real dragons?" Kai snapped.

"I'm extrapolating," she replied testily. "If the scale was here, the logical explanation is that the dragon was as well. No way Ms. Keeper could have managed it to the extent that there were no claw gauges on the floor or scorch marks. Ergo, Ms. Keeper must have been the dragon herself."

"My brainiac," I beamed.

"Why not? The simplest explanation is usually the most logical," Theo agreed, "but we still need to narrow down what type of dragon."

"So Sophie knows how kill it," added Kai.

"Me? Why me?" I asked.

"You seem to care."

I stared at him, dumbfounded. "That was a tasteless joke, right?"

"No," Theo said. "He means it."

"How can anyone be so unfeeling?" Hannah demanded.

Kai looked to Theo for help. "What part of this don't they get?"

"The part where you let innocent people be hurt without trying to save them," I retorted. "What part of that don't you get?"

Theo sighed. "Much as I hate to defend Kai, he's not actually acting like a psychopath. There's a fundamental difference between how humans and gods think."

"Yeah," Kai interjected. "Humans get all upset about the littlest things."

"Littlest things?" Hannah sputtered. "We're talking lives."

"Little picture, sweetheart."

Hannah made an "ugh" of disgust. "Don't 'sweet-heart' me."

Theo tried to placate them both. "It's like this. Humans see the trees, gods see the forest. We're more infinite so our perspective is larger."

Kai brightened. "Exactly." He paused. "I do care about humans. They make great playthings."

I frowned. He didn't have to rub in his hots for Bethany now of all times.

Kai continued. "I don't particularly want to see them destroyed in all this. But you can't be concerned with the survival as a whole and be caught up in each individual sob story. You'd never get anywhere."

"Run along then and go worry about your world dominance," I scoffed. "I'll deal without you." I made a shooing motion.

Kai hesitated.

"Ohmigod." A slow smirk spread across my face. "You can't, can you? That's why you're here. Whatever you were up to involves me. I'm essential to your evil plans, aren't I?"

"You didn't think they were so evil when you were your proper self."

"I am my proper self. With an attitude adjustment." Cassie's gibberish popped into my mind. "I'm the key, aren't I?"

"Don't flatter yourself," Kai said. "It's not all about you."

"Then it's about the two of us," I continued. "Me from above, you from below, together we make a key."

Kai stared at me warily. "How do you know this?"

"Cassie told us," Theo replied. "We figure she's a descendent of the Oracle."

"Why didn't you say something sooner?" Kai demanded.

Was he kidding me? "I did! Back in the bathroom. You wouldn't listen. Too busy with the twisting of words and the kissing and being cryptic."

"She's the one you thought I wanted to harm? She might have had some useful information. Why would I hurt her?"

"Maybe you'd already gotten the information you needed from her, rendering her expendable," Hannah pointed out.

"And maybe you're deluded," Kai retorted.

I had a sick feeling. "It was world domination, wasn't it? I wasn't going to simply stop the war. I was going to take over." I looked at Kai for confirmation. "No," I continued sadly at his look, "*we* were going to take over. That's why you came back? Not because of me or us. Because you needed me to achieve your goals."

"My goals were our goals. Stop being so human about this." Kai sounded genuinely annoyed.

"I hate to say 'I told you so,'" Theo began until Hannah smacked him.

Guess it had been too much to hope that I was merely an unwitting pawn in this battle for world domination. Nope. Little old me was a major player engaged in a coup d'état to usurp the two most powerful gods imaginable. Except, while they still wanted me dead, in true fashion of power mad dictators and gods everywhere, I was no longer major. Bet I hadn't seen that little change in status coming. Big dummy.

I was, however, still key. Both to the battle and to Cassie's plight. This dragon would never have taken Cassie if I hadn't somehow set off her powers. She was the vision-seeing aftershock of my goddess earthquake. Whether intended or not, this was my fault. The enormity of my responsibility hit me full on.

"I'm taking the scale to examine it further," Hannah announced, breaking into my pity party.

"I'll come too," Theo said. "I have an idea about how to break through the ward and the scale is key. Soph, what are you going to do?"

A glimpse of red hair outside the window caught my eye. "Bethany?"

Everyone rushed to look outside.

"Who's she with?" Hannah asked, squinting for a better look.

"She's strolling around pretty casually for someone supposedly abducted by a dragon," Theo commented.

"I'll go talk to her," I said, and raced out the door. I'd been feeling itchy inside and the chance to get outdoors was compelling.

By the time I reached where I'd seen her, Bethany already hopped the fence and was headed into the woods.

Of course.

It was incredibly stupid to follow her outside the protective bubble but I didn't feel like I had a choice. I had to find out if Bethany had escaped Ms. Keeper.

If so, how? Did she know where Cassie was? And yes, was Bethany all right? Her obsessed fangirl Veronica had forgotten her completely, which meant that something wonky was at play.

Plus, time was still ticking for Cassie. I was worried for her life, not to mention the fact that she might be able to clear Theo and I of any wrongdoing where poisoning Hades was involved. And if Cassie knew who had poisoned the Underlord, I might know who tried to kill me.

All things considered, it was a calculated risk I had to take. I climbed cautiously over the fence, touching my pendant for luck and courage.

No Infernorators or Gold Crushers showed up. Hopefully, Hades' change in status was keeping the Underworld busy. And if Zeus thought I was behind it, could be he'd leave me alone.

I continued through the forest, keeping a sharp eye on my former foe up in the distance. I tried calling her name but she didn't appear to hear me.

Even though I was anxious about being ambushed by a variety of deadly supernatural beings, every step deeper into the tangle of trees and further away from people recharged me. While I wasn't at the "dance naked amidst the flowers" stage yet, my almost drool-inducing need to let it all hang out in the outdoors was bordering on severe embarrassment territory. I had my shoes off again and had started to pull up my shirt before I realized what I was doing and restored my clothing. I consoled myself with the feel of autumn sun on my face.

I found Bethany deep in the woods, at the edge of a steep ravine. Or should I say, I found a twelve-year-old wearing my Bethany wig and sneaking a smoke with her friend.

I snatched the lousy wig off her head.

"What's your deal?" she sneered. God, I hated lippy tweens.

"The deal is, that's my wig, which you probably stole from Principal Doucette. Not to mention, smoking kills."

"Yeah, well, you'll be dead before us," her annoying friend piped up. They snickered.

Seriously? I'd risked life and limb to be insulted by a pair of prepubescent brats?

"Not really," I assured them, "I've got this special longevity thing working for me. Do you know what 'longevity' means?"

They exchanged an annoyed glance.

"It means that when your cold bodies are rotting in the grave, I'll be radiantly youthful. And you are going to be rotting sooner rather than later if I ever catch either of you smoking again. Got it?"

Fun fact number one. Goddess pissyness totally terrifies kids. Or they thought I was insane. Either way, they tossed their cigarettes into the ravine and bolted.

"Burn down the whole forest, why dontcha?" I yelled after them. Grumbling, I scrambled and slid my way down the fifty feet to the bottom of the ravine. This Goddess of Spring gig meant a whole new attachment to the earth for me and I couldn't risk their stupid cigarettes accidentally burning down the forest. Bad enough I had the ancient Greek pyromania squad mucking around.

I scuffed my feet through the leaf-strewn ground at the bottom until I found their butts. Sure enough, they were still smoldering. Carefully, I put them out and tried to re-dirtify the area.

Storm clouds darkened the day. I glanced up, hoping the rain would stay off long enough for me to get inside, and realized there were no clouds.

Photokia and Pyrosim filled every inch of sky.

Me against all of them. I gave a grim smile and lashed out.

An eerie calm filled my entire body and I felt as if time slowed down. Infernorators and Gold Crushers descended upon me, fireballs and thunderbolts raining down upon my lone human form.

Yet I had plenty of time to avoid them. I brushed their destruction away like I was swatting flies. My stranglers spun about me in a blur. I laughed in sheer delight as I realized that I'd only been using a fraction of my power.

I. Was. Spring.

The time when life begins anew. I had all the elemental power that came with the season. Even now, in Fall, I was able to call upon it. I felt it surge up from deep within its sleeping place in the earth and blast from my eyes in a deadly green light.

I may have been the embodiment of the season when life began to grow anew, but I had the ability to push that power to the extreme. Pervert and twist it so that my attackers grew so fast, they hit the other side of existence.

This is what they'd meant when they said humans see the trees and gods see the forest. Big picture. Attacking my enemies one by one would only get me so far. It was a fraction of what I was capable of.

Power consumed me and shot from my eyes and palms in waves of moss green light, taking out row upon row of the deadly minions. I watched them age into nothingness, then disappear from existence.

I was unstoppable. Every inch of me was pure might.

I remembered this rush. More so, in fact.

I was on an island. No, not even that. More of a rocky outcropping in the middle of a turquoise blue sea that stretched as far as the eye could see. I lay on my back, the rock smooth and cool against my skin.

Kai propped himself on his elbows, his body stretched above me. He touched his forehead to mine and I was consumed with energy. All became light. I could see the world broken down into its tiniest fragments. Together we were the creator and the destroyer. Together, all was ours.

I rushed back to the present with a snap. While my mind had drifted back into the past, my body had stayed present and focused, continuing its battle.

This. Was. Amazing.

Then I learned a valuable lesson. Like all power sources, I needed to be recharged. I had thought that because I was outside, the superpowers would be indefinite.

Not so, kids.

Apparently there was a limit on how much I could extend myself in any one session.

You know that moment in movies when the heroes

are deep in it, guns firing away, and there's that click? That super loud click, when all other sound seems to have stopped, that shows the hero has run out?

That's what happened to me. One moment I was single-handedly decimating an otherworldly army, the next I was a puny human with a legion of foes bent on killing me. From one second to the next, my powers stopped and I stood there in defenseless disbelief.

I wasn't the only one. There was a moment—it felt like minutes but must have been milliseconds—where I stared at my enemies and they all stared back. We had mutually frozen in stunned shock.

Looking back, I'm amazed I wasn't killed. I was hideously outnumbered and for every being I'd taken out, ten more had shown up to take its place.

I closed my eyes as fire and lightning engulfed me. I could feel my skin sizzle as I spasmed violently from the electricity arcing over my body.

Something seized my shirt front. Dazed, my eyes struggled open to find a scarred Gold Crusher holding me in his grasp. He smiled, revealing his snaggle teeth. All I could think was "I guess Zeus doesn't provide dental care."

Both the Crusher's eyes and his thunderbolt tattoo glowed with an otherworldly eeriness. He flew up in the air, my body clutched firmly to him like a child with his favorite teddy. No one was getting me away from him.

Whoops. Spoke too soon. A lone Infernorator swooped down upon us and used his flaming tentacle to knock the Crusher sideways so hard, my teeth rattled.

The two foes attacked each other. Fire met lightning and the sky exploded in red and gold, as they made their hatred plain.

I wasn't sure who I wanted to win. I guess the Photokia. Better the devil already holding you and all that.

I got my wish soon enough. My captor hurtled his fiery foe into a Sitka spruce with enough force to cause an impressive Underworldy fireball.

My hero.

Problem was, then his attention turned back to the prize in his hand. Me.

"Pretty," he leered, reaching for my pendant.

Over my dead body was he getting it. I reached far inside myself, beyond the pain, beyond the exhaustion. I was ending this *now*.

Something in the recesses of my brain that pre-dated my human consciousness stirred. A primeval force that had been sleeping, waiting for the command to "awake."

I hesitated. I knew instinctively that tapping into that force meant there was no going back. I could never hide behind human ignorance again. To drink from this source was to fully commit; to my goddess nature, to the war, and to my birthright.

I chose.

Finally.

The dental nightmare squeezing me placed one hand on my pendant. "Wonder what Zeus will give me for this?" he laughed, oozing foul breath.

Bzzz. So sorry. The correct answer was "What righteous babe is about to blow you to smithereens?"

Fully, irreversibly, finally, totally me. I closed my eyes, then girlfriend gave 'er. Light blasted out from my entire body. The world around me trembled with the muted boom of my all-encompassing shockwave.

My eyes cracked open. Dazzling blue. The sky was clear. My enemies gone.

Any leaves that had been clinging to their branches were now on the ground, dead.

I knew that they wouldn't be enough to cushion me.

Because I was falling. And so tired. My human tupperware exterior could still get cracked. Needed to remember that for next time.

I hurtled downward. My hands burned like a mother, and after that hailstorm of electric shocks, my head felt like it was only semi-attached. A rib or two might have been broken as well. On a scale of one to ten, I'd cranked the pain to eleven.

The ground rushed toward me and I remembered enough about physics to know that when I landed, it was going to hurt. A lot. Theo's comment about how sometimes death was a blessing popped into my head. Now might be one of those times.

This was it. Five, four, three, two … I heard the ground beneath me rumble as if something had landed on it, hard. Was it me?

"Like I said," Kai's voice rumbled against my chest as he caught me safe in his arms, "a walking suicide mission."

My brain, barely working at all by this point, couldn't even form the words to ask where he'd come from. The only way down to this spot was from the top of the ravine. I looked up at it, confused.

Kai must have read my thoughts because he grinned and said "I like to jump." Then he proved that point with a running leap, soaring up the fifty feet to the top of the ravine.

That got my attention. I processed it.

Then I blacked out.

When I came to, I was back in my bed. Hannah was bundled in her bathrobe, hovering over me, terrified. I tried to smile reassuringly. Instead I blacked out again.

The second time I came to, Kai was sitting on the edge of my bed, frowning. "Some death wish you've got."

I rolled over, too tired to engage. "Some bedside manner. Go away. I want Hannah."

"She had to go to class."

"Don't you?" I asked, not really caring.

"Why? Because if I flunk out I can't get into university and make something of myself?"

Good point. "How long was I out?"

"A day."

Tentatively, I took stock of my condition. Toes wiggling. Check. Neck moving. Check. Arms?

I lifted my hands. They peeked out from under my too-long pajama sleeves, bandaged in heavy gauze. I panicked as I realized that part of my head was bandaged as well. I had to get to a mirror and see if I was hideously deformed by burns.

I struggled to sit up.

"Where do you think you're going?" Kai asked.

"Mirror." I needed all my energy to prop myself up.

Kai gently pushed me back down. "No," he said.

I fought him as best I could. "Let me up."

"As imperious as always," he muttered, keeping me firmly in place.

That surprised me. "I would have thought I was a lovely goddess. Everyone likes Spring."

"Yeah," he said, in voice that sounded oddly sarcastic, "you were a real doll."

I closed my eyes. "I'm going to make children cry now, aren't I?"

He laughed. A rich belly laugh. I refused to think about what the sound did to me. I was hurt, not aroused. If I reminded myself of that about fifty thousand times, I might believe it.

My eyes snapped open. "Do I amuse you?"

"Annoy, actually, but I'm trying to focus on the positive." He shot me an angelic smile.

"Are you going to help me up?"

"No. You have a broken rib, your hands are badly burned, and your head was singed."

"Not my face?"

"Nope. You lost some hair. It'll grow back, and the burns on your scalp will heal. Theo doctored you. Meantime, you stay put."

"You like the fact that I'm stuck here at your mercy. You like the indignity of it."

"It's an added bonus. Yeah."

I voiced the question that had been bothering me. "Why didn't they kill me? They had the chance."

"You're wanted alive."

I doubted it was so we could have tea. The big bosses probably wanted to kill me themselves. "But they attacked. If I was to be taken alive, why all of the pyrotechnics?"

"Alive doesn't preclude having a little fun first."

"Like how a lion toys with a gazelle before ripping its throat, fun?"

When Kai stared at me, incredulous, I shrugged. "I spend a lot of time with Hannah. She's very vocal about her interests. Wait. Is the school wondering what happened to me? Or have I disappeared from memory, too?"

"Hannah put it out that you have food poisoning and need a couple days to recover."

"It's going to take more than that."

He shook his head. "Doubtful. You get beat up easier than you did as Persephone but you heal faster than a normal human."

Only because I wasn't dead. "Thank you. For saving me from splattage."

"You were pretty impressive," he admitted. "Couldn't let that go to waste."

I allowed myself a small smirk. "Yeah. I kicked their asses."

"You did. Looks like you're up to speed on your power."

I was. Faulty still on the memories, though, which made talking to Kai a constant battle between doubt and desire.

"Now you just need to master defying gravity and

176

you'll be good to go." He grinned at me and I felt myself falling into that smile.

Cue cheesy music as our eyes locked.

This wasn't "Sweet Valley High." Some piece of Kai's true form had emerged, because when I gazed into his eyes, I saw something not-quite-human staring back at me. It was ancient and feral.

Something inside me flickered in recognition. I tamped down hard on it. Evidently, I hadn't really thought through all the consequences of embracing that Greek heritage of mine. When it came to love lives, those gods made cable seem tame.

I, Sophie Bloom, the girl who had barely been kissed, was *so* out of her league. I laughed. Hard. Possibly with a touch of hysteria.

Kai stared at me, puzzled. "I've never heard you really laugh."

That seemed wrong. "Didn't I have a sense of humor?"

He thought about it. "I guess so. But you would never have let yourself go like that. Too concerned about appearance."

"I was vain?" Super weird idea.

"All goddesses are vain. Goes with their beauty."

"Score points for that."

"They're not mouthy though. Not like you. You always say what you think. Gods and goddesses tend to be more crafty. They'll strike out at you, but under the facade of seeming so pleasant. A smile to your face and a knife to your back."

"Majorly sucky way to live."

He shrugged. "It is what it is."

He stretched out his arms, fingers intertwined, palms outward. A tiny scar in the hollow between his thumb and forefinger caught my attention. I took his hand and ran my finger over it. "I remember that. How did you transfer it to your human form?"

"I'm not human. What you see is what you get." He tugged his hand away to frown at his scar.

I felt the loss. "No. You're waaaay taller."

"I've dialed my energy down to fit in. We never appear on earth in our true form."

Maybe, but I sensed a caginess about him. "You're holding out on me." He remained silent. "Oh, come on. I'll get better faster if you tell me."

"That's scientific."

"Fine. I'll nag you til you do." I curled my fingers into my palms, resisting the urge to touch him again.

His lips compressed in a thin line, like he was suppressing a smile. "Guess it can't do any harm for you to know. I couldn't cross Theo's wards in my true form. Even though I bore no active intention to harm, my life force was too strong. I had to dampen it."

"That's why Ms. Keeper couldn't come through all dragony."

"Yeah. She had to assume a less potent form."

"So, if you unveiled yourself to me?"

"I'd blow your little mind. I'm still myself. Not human. Just reigned in."

It made sense, especially given what I'd seen in his

eyes. For the first time, I truly believed he was a god. Not just intellectually understood it, but knew it.

A question nagged at me. "How did Theo? Become human, I mean."

"Dark magic. I don't know why he'd …" He trailed off.

I poked him as a prompt.

"Dark magic demands a price. A high one."

"So?"

"Well, two of you were made human, weren't you?"

"You mean the price of turning me human was Theo becoming human, too? Why would anyone demand that of him?"

Kai looked at me fondly. Like I was an idiot child to be tolerated. "Beings that practice that type of sorcery aren't nice. Could be spite. Because they could. Or because they wanted his god essence—his powers—and gave him a human shell to house what was left. You'd have to ask him."

No wonder Theo had been so dodgy to Hannah and me about taking on his true form. This was awful. He'd paid too high a price.

"You won't fail him," Kai said.

I hated that he could so easily read me. "How can you know that?"

"Don't really have a choice, do you? If you want to make it right for him, you have to save humanity. To do that, you have to stop the war on earth."

"And to do that, I have to help you take over."

He smoothed away a strand of hair that had fallen in my face. "Would it be so bad?"

I tried not to shiver under his gentle touch. "Don't know. No idea what it entails. Don't even know how we do it." Nervously, I smoothed my comforter.

He tucked the strand behind my ear and leaned in close. "Two become one."

It took a minute for the penny to drop. "Sex?!"

Disappointment flickered in Kai's eyes. I guess my incredulous tone of voice hurt his poor ego.

"Yeah, sex," he said flatly, moving back. "Big bang, honey."

"Ahhh!" I covered my ears, embarrassed. Yes, and fascinated. "I thought we touched foreheads."

Kai shrugged. "If that's some kind of euphemism for orgasm, then sure. We touched foreheads."

I swatted him away. "You know, maybe goddesses don't care, but a girl likes a gesture or two before she hops into bed with someone."

"No bed," he pointed out. "It was always outdoors for you."

I steeled myself against the deliciously naughty images running through my head and tried to stay on point. "Gestures like flowers. Or chocolates. Maybe even a date to actually get to know the guy, before she just gives it up."

Kai swore. "Give it up? Are you a virgin?" Said like it was leprosy.

"Yes." I jutted my chin out. "Got a problem with it?"

"In general, yes." He sighed heavily. "Guess I'll have to take one for the team."

"Presuming it's you, smart guy." .

He didn't look pleased at that. "It will be."

"That a threat?"

"Just a fact, Sophie Bloom. Don't play jealousy games with a god."

He got up and stalked off.

Well, at least he'd be jealous.

I dished to Hannah later that evening. She supported me in feeling this was one giant heap of messed up as she led me through some kind of "follow the light" test with a flashlight to assure herself I didn't have a concussion.

I humored her and tried not to stare too hard at the vertigo-inducing fractal pattern on her T-shirt.

"There's enough pressure around your first time without having the fate of the universe depending on it." She swung the flashlight. "Look up."

A wise woman. "I know, right? And what if it's bad? Does that mean I only save half the population? This would be a lot easier if I'd already had sex. It wouldn't seem so huge."

"Think of it as simple biological urges. Although, you could totally cat around in the meantime." She clicked off the flashlight, apparently satisfied with her findings.

"Kai wasn't too on board with that idea."

"You're gonna let him dictate what you can do with your body?"

I cut her off before I bore the brunt of her feminist

outrage. "Down girl. I agree with you. Thing is, it's not like there's any other guy I want to have sex with."

Hannah narrowed her eyes at me. "Any other? Meaning you want to have sex with *him*?"

"I have. As Persephone."

"Past tense, pussycat. Would you sleep with him now?"

I fluffed up my pillows. Avoidance tactic. Would I? The thought was exciting and scary and overwhelming to me in my weakened state.

Hannah cleared her throat. "I'm waiting."

"I'm not ready to sleep with anyone. But what if I don't? And I miss my chance to do whatever it is I'm supposed to?"

"As a representative of the human race, that would suck for us."

"I'm human, too."

"Only marginally. I don't senior citizen things to death when I get mad," she pointed out.

"Don't forget my glowing eyes of fury."

"Making your freakiness complete."

I bowed best I could being propped up against pillows. "I pride myself on being well-rounded."

Hannah crossed the room to put the flashlight away in her desk drawer. "Seems to me that you're going to need more information. How is this whole power dealie supposed to go down? When? Where? And what does it mean for us mere mortals?"

"Agreed. But Kai isn't the greatest with the sharing of info."

"Talk to Theo," Hannah replied.

"Are you crazy? He already hates Kai. Plus, he's like my brother and I so am not having a detailed sex chat with him. Also, he might not know. I doubt Kai and I were going around sharing these details. And if other gods knew we could do this, they would have tried to …" Oh.

Hannah completed my thought. "Kill you. Makes you wonder who else knew what was going on when you were god-slaughtered."

"And why Hades and Zeus came to finish the job. It might not be because they think I tricked them and have gone human. Maybe they don't want me to carry out my plans."

"Theo says that Hades is still incapacitated from the poison. You know, the event you failed to mention that you'd been framed for?"

I scowled. "I didn't want you to know. You'd worry."

"No kidding," she said, gently swatting the top of my head. "But you still suck for not telling me. Anyhow, apparently the odd couple, Death and Sleep, seem to be running the show. Since they don't love you, either, absolutely do not leave the grounds. Even if it seems like the right thing to do. At least not without Theo's say-so. Promise?"

"Promise. Do you remember anything about Cassie?"

Hannah looked at me, with no trace of understanding.

"Never mind," I said. I had my answer. "We'll get her back from Ms. Keeper."

"Who?"

Beyond a vague curiosity, Hannah didn't even seem

to care that much that we were discussing people she no longer remembered. Memory loss side effect, perhaps? "No way. Now you don't remember her, either?" Keeper was a master of memory loss. "She's a dragon? You found her scale."

Her eyes glinted in interest. "Where is it?"

"Theo has it. Needed for magic, not dissection. Okay. Here's the deal. Ms. Keeper, our phony guidance counselor, is probably a dragon. We think she's made everyone forget about two students she's abducted and has now probably made you all forget her existence so that she can go carry out her evil plans."

"Impressive."

"No. Dangerous. You need to stay far away from her." I snapped my fingers. "Pen."

"Yes, master," Hannah grumbled, handing me a felt.

I grabbed her palm and wrote the word "Keeper" on it. Then I circled it and put a slash through it. "Keeper bad. Don't let this fade. It's your reminder. Like 'keep out.'"

"Got it. I don't like Ms. Keeper. But can I have her scale when we're done?"

"No."

She pouted.

"Fine."

She clapped her hands in delight.

I didn't want to kill her happy buzz, but if I didn't figure out how to stop the dragon from taking down our entire student body, Hannah could end up close and personal with a lot more than the scale.

10
You can lead a nymph to water but you cannot make her think

ι′

I had pretty much slept for three days straight and to my surprise, Kai was right. I was healed. This was good news for me but bad for Cassie and Bethany. It meant I'd lost precious time in the quest to save them and had to step things up.

Much as I chafed at any delay, I had my own immediate problem to deal with. My little heal-a-thon meant that I was now way behind on my schoolwork, with exams and essay deadlines looming. To blow them off would be at my peril, a decree handed down to me by Principal Doucette my first morning up and around.

"Given your probationary status," he began in a low rumbling drone, "it is imperative that you honor your commitments if you wish to remain a student here at Hope Park."

I won't bore you with the rest of that speech, which invoked school pride, calling Felicia, and a glimpse of a life that involved me waiting tables. Poor guy was trying to scare me into pulling up those university-bound boot-straps, and all he succeeded in doing was painting a rosy picture of a future where my biggest concern was that no one stiffed me on the bill.

If only it was as simple as popping a wad of gum in my mouth, teasing my hair, and hitting the nearest truck stop café. That combustible experience back at the ravine had cemented the fact that I was not yet ready to take on all the forces of Zeus and Hades singlehandedly. I was definitely stronger and more capable, but for now, staying in the Hope Park bubble was a no-brainer.

The one-on-one time between me and the principal did enable me to discover that he had no memory of Ms. Keeper, either. I pressed him on it, even going so far as to take him to her office, but he couldn't even acknowledge its existence. His eyes just slid off it and he went blank.

"She's our guidance counselor. Took over from Mrs. Rivers?"

"Mrs. who?"

He didn't remember Mrs. Rivers. That was a blow.

I knew that the family emergency that she'd been called away on was a sham, but the fact that Keeper had bothered to make people forget her very existence did not bode well. Just one more person to add to my guilty conscience.

However, since I couldn't save anyone if I got myself expelled and killed without my safe zone, honor my commitments I did. As fast as possible. However, I had not forgotten my responsibilities.

As with any good leader, I delegated. In part, to Mr. Smarty Pants "never study, get all A's" Theo Rockman. His secret, I now knew, was longevity. Stick around for millennia and high school curricula became blindingly easy.

I demanded continual updates on how his ward-cracking attempts were going.

I had Hannah confirm that neither the Rivers nor Jones family had any idea they were missing loved ones, or even that they had loved ones to miss. Yeah, shoot me. I didn't bother checking in with Bethany's family. I may have felt it my duty to get Bethany back, but that didn't mean I missed her.

Bad as it was that Hannah didn't remember Bethany or Cassie, it was heartbreaking that she'd forgotten the existence of one of her favorite staff.

Meantime, I also had to keep the remaining students safe from Ms. Keeper, in case she decided to take anyone else out.

Since I couldn't patrol the grounds 24/7, I came up with a plan to let my schoolmates do it for me.

I photocopied flyers of my "Keeper—Keep Out" symbol and circulated them around the school. It described her human form and warned students that if they saw her, to stay far away but tell me immediately. I conned everyone into thinking it was part of an interactive drama project. The flyers promised candy to whoever found her first. Hopefully, my student alarm force would work.

I spent the next several days glued to a cubicle seat in the library. I even stayed focused, only taking the occasional thousand glances or so out the window. First up?

A ten page paper on Shakespeare's ill-fated love between Romeo and Juliet.

Talk about timing. Or was it irony? The jury was still out on Kai and me, but the way things were going, Romeo and Juliet had a Disney ending compared to us. While our history didn't involve a well-meaning priest, I wasn't ruling out some goat-horned shaman dropping in at any time. Feuding families, star-crossed lovers, and death and deception. There were enough similarities in our stories to put me off old Billy S. for good.

Somewhere between writer's cramp and cramming, I slept. Not a restful snuggle-into-the-covers refresher, but a lay-face-down-on-my-study-table-and-drool, glorified nap.

Bless Hannah. She pimped me food and made sure I maintained a socially acceptable level of hygiene.

Wednesday afternoon, all papers in and exams taken, I got changed for what had previously been my biggest nightmare—gym class. Now it was my last chance to touch base with Theo and Hannah before going to find Keeper. To once and for all put everything into place.

Our teacher, Mr. Naiman, was one of those disgustingly robust types that never got sick, and proclaimed fresh air to be good for every ailment under the sun. The fact that the sun would be hard-pressed to fight its way through the gloomy November cloud cover mattered not.

Shivering in our sweats and hoodies, most of the class grumbled their way outside, following him as he took loud, deep breaths and led us in an energetic sprint to warm us up.

Last week, I would have been the grumpiest. Today, I burst through the door in a gleeful bound.

"What's wrong with you?" Hannah's confusion was understandable.

The look on her face as I picked up a pine cone and tossed it at her was priceless. "Nature, baby. Race you to the track."

"Oddess-gay o-fay ing-spray," Theo clarified as they caught up.

"She's manic and sunny," Hannah muttered. "It's scaring me."

"Roll out, kitten." I slapped Hannah's butt and broke into a brisk jog.

As we ran in the fabulously fresh air, we reviewed our findings and discussed our plan of attack. I hoped that the more Hannah heard about it, the more it would reinforce that Ms. Keeper was a danger and prevent further memory loss in case she resurfaced.

"The good news," Theo began, checking over his shoulder to ensure no one was too near, "is that I don't think Cassie is dead. I believe that Keeper won't show up until she's completed whatever task she has set for herself. And given her interest in Cassie, Keeper seems to need her participation. So for now, at least, Cassie is probably safe."

A knot of tension I didn't realize I'd been carrying loosened. I crossed my fingers and hoped the good fortune extended to Bethany and Mrs. Rivers as well.

"That's good," said Hannah. "I wouldn't want anything to happen to her."

189

"You remember?" I was delighted.

Hannah blushed and pulled a cue card out of her of hoodie pocket. "Theo helped me write everything down so I'd be in the loop. I've memorized facts about them. Like they're an English assignment, not real." She paused. "I'm sorry I don't remember them, though."

"So where are they?"

Theo pushed his glasses back up his nose. "Not sure."

Huh. "Okay, if she's not dead, what happened while we were in Hades to make everyone forget about her?"

"No clue."

I fixed Theo with a disapproving look. "You're wowing me with mediocrity."

"Get stuffed," he replied smoothly. "You're asking the wrong questions. What you should be asking is 'who took Cassie?'"

"Who took Cassie?" Hannah asked obediently.

"Hey, Bloom! I mean, Sophie."

I startled, not having realized Anil had arrived and worried about what he might have overheard.

"Hey, Anil." I glanced over at Hannah and Theo for enlightenment on this jovial salutation but merely got an indifferent shrug from Theo and a smirk from Hannah. So no help there.

"Feeling better?" he inquired solicitously.

This was getting weirder and weirder. "Fine, thanks."

"Cool. Cool. What'd you think of that bio exam? Brutal, huh?"

Hannah smothered a laugh.

It dawned on me that Anil was attempting to chat

me up. In a blatantly unsupportive act, my former best friends jogged ahead, as if to give us some privacy.

Thanks a bunch.

I consoled myself with the thought that I really could kill them. Not that I'd ever do that. (And *Psycho* violins play ... now.)

Anil was still waiting for me to answer. I opened my mouth to blow him off as per our usual discourse. "The dissection was pretty fun." Apparently, some latent manners had just kicked in.

"Did you hear about Jackson's eyeball?" He then proceeded to regale me with a hilarious story about Jackson squirting eye fluid during his dissection exam.

I found myself laughing. And dare I admit it, kind of flirting back. When Anil wasn't being a total meathead, which was most of my past association with him, he was kind of cute. He had beautiful brown skin and darkly fringed eyes. A solid grin, too. It was nice. Normal.

I sighed. Normal was not in my cards. At least, not until I'd resolved the immediate crisis at hand. I had to finish talking to Theo. "I should probably find Larry and Moe and go stretch."

He nodded. "Sure. Catch you later?"

I meant to say, "Sorry, no." Had a list of reasons why not, including how shallow he was to only start noticing me in my new, improved Sophie form, but I couldn't blame him. He was just a regular teenaged guy who'd never done anything worse to me than mouth off and get mouthed off at in return. I didn't want to lead him on but I wasn't going to be a bitch either. "For sure. We'll always have eyeball dissections."

He grinned and jogged off.

I went and found my turncoat friends, who greeted me with kissy noises. "Perhaps we should be focusing on the important issues at hand," I retorted loftily. "Who's behind this?" I asked Theo.

"All scales point to Delphyne," he replied with triumphant finality.

I glanced at Hannah, who shook her head.

"Theo, while I'm thrilled you've figured it out, we have no idea who that is." We completed our final lap and headed for the grassy area where kids had started to cool down.

"You've got to learn your basic Greek history."

"I'll do that with all my free time. Cheat sheet, please?"

He humphed. "Delphyne is a dragon who used to guard the Oracle at Delphi."

"Where Cassandra was," Hannah said.

"Clever girl." He bestowed a pleased smile on her.

"So why is she here?" I still was missing the big picture.

"For Cassie, obviously."

We stood there, lamely stretching but mostly chatting. "Obvious how? To do what?"

He looked a little less certain. "You know. Cassie foretells things. Delphyne guarded the Oracle."

"Still not making the connection."

"The 'why' of it is still a tad unclear," he admitted.

"Less talking, more stretching," Mr. Naiman called

over to us. We lowered our voices and followed directions.

I turned to Theo. "Can Delphyne be killed?"

"Mos' def."

There had to be a catch. "We need a magic bow dipped
in poison and forged by an elf chained to a tree on Mt.
Olympus?" I asked, attemping to keep my balance as I
stetched out my right thigh by bringing my foot back to
touch my butt.

"No elves," Theo said. "You're reading all the wrong
books. The poison has possibilities, though. Gorgon's
blood would be brilliant."

"No problem." I turned to Hannah. "I think Mrs.
Singh has some in the lab."

Theo shot a look of contempt my way.

"Where do we find a Gorgon and how do we convince
it to give up its poison?" Hannah cut to the chase as she
dropped into a lunge stretch.

"It's not so much a bargaining process as a killing
process," Theo explained. "That, or we need to get close
enough to nick her left side and get a drop of her blood."

"Why left?" Hannah didn't seem to make the distinction. I sure didn't.

Theo sat on the ground and stretched forward toward
his feet. "Because the blood of a Gorgon's right side
brings people back to life and her left kills people."

"How very yin and yang," Hannah murmured, shaking out her shoulders.

"It's hopeless." I steeled myself to begin the grieving
process for Cassie.

"Ye of little faith." Theo shook his head at us. "We're not going to have to get anywhere near a Gorgon because I have another way. Check it, yeah? I've got a source."

We stood up and followed Mr. Naiman back toward the gym.

I could only begin to imagine. "Let me guess. This fatal poison is what was used on both Hades and me. But it stays in the blood for a long time, so we sneak back to the Underworld, acquire Hades' blood with said poison still in it, put it on some sort of stabby thing and presto. Dragon be gone."

Theo looked at me with admiration. "I was thinking that you could use your persuasive charms on Kai to get it for us."

"Get bent." I retorted.

"I'm kind of impressed with how you figured that all out," Hannah said.

"I'll tell you." Theo beckoned her close. "It's because it's a load of rubbish. Sophie's twisted mind running rampant with neuroses."

"Tabling the fact that you're a jerk for that Kai crack, I wasn't poisoned with Gorgon blood?"

"No way. That stuff is instantly fatal. I wouldn't have had any time to put your soul anywhere. By the time I found you, it would have been too late."

"That was stupid. Why poison me with something on a timer? It's like those villains who spill their entire plan to the hero, giving them time to get away."

"If I ever decide to poison you, I promise I'll make sure your demise is instant," he replied. "Remember, when we got back from Hades, I told you the knife you'd been stabbed with was enchanted. Whoever cut you didn't just want you dead. They wanted you to suffer, as well. It was a fluke I was even there. No one knew I was supposed to meet with your mother." He thought about it a moment. "Come to think of it, the palace was oddly empty, which meant that some kind of diversion had been arranged. Ask Kai about that one."

"And Hades?" Hannah asked. "Why take the chance that having him suffer would foul up his death?"

"Hades is one of the big three, along with Zeus and Poseidon. I'm not positive that even Gorgon blood would be instantly fatal to him. It would take something massive to off them. In all my years, I've never come across anything that could do the job."

Hannah bounced up and down excitedly as she walked. "Then it was a message. Someone showing that they could get to him. Make him vulnerable and worried. Maybe the seeds were a gift? Like a pair of gloves, but the insides were lined with crushed glass and poison so the wearer put them on and bam! Snuffed out." At our curious expressions, Hannah shrugged. "I've been reading a lot about the Borgias."

"Sure thing, psycho. Who's your source for the Gorgon blood, Theo?"

"No one. We're not using Gorgon blood."

"But you said—"

"I said it would be brilliant. I also said I had another way. To kill Delphyne. Not sure why you're so obsessed with Gorgons."

"Tell me the way," I said wearily, stepping back into the smelly warmth of the gym.

"You. Shouldn't be much of a problem to take her out."

"Aim for the eyes or the soft underbelly," Hannah added thoughtfully. "Those are your best targets."

"It can't be that simple," I protested.

"You're a real cynic, aren't you?" Theo rolled his eyes at the look I shot him. "Fine. There is the matter of the box."

"There we go. What box?"

"The enchanted one. For Delphyne's head. After you decapitate her."

I felt queasy. Killing with my awesome powers from afar, excellent. Getting up close and personal to saw through something? Not so much. "I need to cut off her head?"

"After she's dead. See, Apollo already killed her once."

"And yet she's here. That bodes well," I snarked.

"His problem," Theo continued ignoring me, "was that he didn't properly finish her off."

"You have that in common." Hannah smiled brightly at me.

"Yeah. Some things just don't have the common courtesy to stay dead," Theo agreed.

"I think we have you to blame for Sophie," Hannah pointed out to him. "I could have had a lovely roommate all these years. Maybe with a boat. I always wanted a friend with a boat."

"See if I save you, Nygard. Where do we find this box?"

Mr. Naiman gave a sharp blast on his whistle.

"Stations, people! One minute vigorous activity for each exercise. On my count."

"Nysa. A nymph," Theo replied as we made for the hand weights.

He was looking at me expectantly. I called him on it. "Am I supposed to know her?"

"Yeah. Wondering if you remembered her."

"Sorry. I'm sure she's very nice," I said, picking up a couple of five-pounders.

Theo picked up a set of ten pound weights and laughed as Mr. Naiman blew his whistle.

We met Theo's very nice nymph at 2am the next morning. "She some kind of vampire nymph? Can't keep daylight hours?" I was tired, shivering despite the many layers of sweatclothes under my jacket, and would have liked just one Greek figure to behave normally.

I was also somewhat edgy since we were waiting near the bank of the creek and even though Theo had assured me a thousand times that the portal was safely shut, I continually worried that Cerberus was going to poke his triple-headed ugly mug out and finish me.

One worry led me to another and soon I was thinking about what Theo had given up. "Do you ever miss it?"

He stared off into the sky, up at the few visible stars. I worried that maybe I'd overstepped and he wasn't going to answer, but after a moment he looked at me. "You know how people who've had limbs amputated can still feel them? Phantom limbs. They itch and they tingle and the person swears that arm or whatever is still there?"

I nodded.

"I swear I can still feel that part of me. Sixteen years since I was a Titan, and every single day I wake with a moment of dread and shock at what I've lost."

"Then why?"

"Because when you've been around forever, you have to find something outside yourself to believe in or go mad. I believe in humanity. I believe in you."

My palms were sweaty and my heart was racing. "What if I'm not worth it?"

"You have to be." He gave me a crooked grin. "Because you're going to have to compensate for Kai."

Well, if Theo could joke, maybe the situation wasn't totally bleak.

The creek began to shimmer. Instinctively, I took a step back, placing Theo square between me and the water. A form rose gracefully from the surface.

Nysa was everything one might expect of a nymph. Slender, with waist length auburn ringlets and large blue eyes, her skin was creamy white. Basically, she was gorgeous.

Unfair! I punched Theo who turned confused eyes my way. "Next time," I hissed "prepare me so I can dress appropriately." I'd never been a girl to care about keeping up with the Jones', but sheesh! Sweats versus the dazzlingness of a nymph was a little too unbalanced, even for me. All I needed to complete the moment was Kai showing up.

I tensed, unsure of how to greet such a spectacular creature and thinking of possible formal salutations. Then she opened her mouth.

"Ahhhhhh" she squealed. "Oh my goddess, I can't even believe it's you!" She bopped out of the river—clad only in some strategically placed seaweed—and rushed me like a twelve-year-old girl reunited with her BFF at summer camp.

She jumped up and down as she clenched me in a hug. Squashed, I looked past her to Theo, who was lamely attempting to keep his composure.

"Like, I can't even believe you're here? When I heard from Prometheus, I was all 'no way.' But he was like 'way.' And he's such a serious ninny that I totally knew he wasn't lying."

That description of Theo so failed to resonate with me that I made a mental note to learn whatever I could about Prometheus. Turning human must have entailed a massive personality switch.

Nysa hadn't stopped talking this entire time. "... She was being such a Medusa head about letting me come. We both knew it was about that seriously cute shepherd liking me and not her. So. Not. My. Fault." She tossed her hair. "I can't help being beautiful." Nysa screeched again. "I love your new size. You used to be so tall, but now ..." She pranced around me in a gleeful jig. "We're the same height. It's like we're sisters!" She poked my padded (99% clothing, 1% chocolate) belly. "'Cept I'm the skinny one!"

Nysa threaded her arm through mine and waited. I had no idea what for. "Uh, yeah."

Apparently that was enough because she jumped up and down. "Whaddya wanna do first?"

"Get the box?"

She stopped jumping and turned a very displeased frown on me. I rushed on. "Please. We're under a kind of tight timeline."

The creek water bubbled. I glanced at it nervously. "And there are a few people who need to be saved."

Steam rose off the water. Nysa glowered at me with full-on hatred. "You haven't seen me in sixteen years and all you can say is you want the box?"

I had the strongest sense that should I say the wrong thing, she might cause my blood to bubble. Time to switch gears. I tossed my hair in my best Bethany imitation and fake laughed. "Just to get the stupid thing out of the way, silly. Theo—Prometheus is so uptight about it. Mr. Stick-up-his-butt."

Theo glared at me, but it was the least he deserved. It was also the right thing to say because Nysa brightened and slapped her forehead. "You. Are. So. Right." She retrieve a small black plastic cube from the creek and tossed it to Theo. It didn't look big enough to hold a finger, much less an entire head. "Scram, boy. This is girlfriend only time."

"Wouldn't dream of impinging," he said, a big smile on his face.

The look I fired back at him promised tortures galore. He was going to leave me with this mentally unstable, dangerous child? I sighed. Fine. I'd give Nysa half an hour and then beg off.

"What now?" I asked brightly.

"Kyrillos." She giggled. "Spill."

I thought it was going to be a very long half hour.

I was so wrong. It was a very long six hours. She made me tell her every detail of my life, then regaled me with her share of sixteen years worth of gossip involving total strangers. Supposedly, I'd known them at some point and should have had a shred of interest. It made reality television seem deep. I couldn't believe I'd cared about it all, at any point.

Somewhere during my third seaweed wrap at the makeshift spa Nysa had set up creekside, as she prattled on about the ongoing saga between Aphrodite and her latest boy toy, I zoned out. I was exhausted, hungry, numb, and suffering from a blinding migraine. If I didn't get away from Nysa and her mindless chattering soon, I was going to turn my powers on myself, end my suffering, and let the human race fend for itself.

I rose and shook off the seaweed. "This has been so super swell but I have to get ready for class." Nysa stared at me like I was an idiot.

"But, like, you're a goddess."

"In human form."

"No probs. I'll come with." Her eyes shone with fervent eagerness. Yeah. That would be great. She could swan into Hope Park mostly naked and I'd pass her off as my cousin. I'm sure no one would mind.

"Are there a lot of cuties?"

That finished it for me. There was already a dragon loose at Hope Park. No nympho nymphs needed. We were full up.

"Nysa." It was my most placating tone.

The creek began to boil again.

"Nysa," I tried again, ignoring the unnatural bubbles frothing in the creek bed. "We can hang another time. Soon. But I really need to go and I'm sure you're being missed and—"

"I'm not finished with you yet!" Huh. More banshee than nymph on that one.

She turned to me with wild eyes, enraged. "You can't tell me what to do! No one tells me what to do. I call the shots!" Before I knew what was happening, she'd wrapped her fingers around my throat and was trying to choke me.

Bless those wards. I definitely had to compliment Theo on a job well done. The second she squeezed my neck, she was flung back violently onto the ground.

"Ouch," she whined. "Whatcha you do that for, huh?"

I wagged my finger at her, parent style. "You tried to choke me. No hurting the goddess."

Her bottom lip quivered. "You don't want to play anymore."

"I'm sure we had this problem before. What happened when I wanted you to leave?"

"I never left."

"You must have left at some point." There was no way I left this running tap of crazy on around me 24/7.

"We played Hide and Seek. I hid and you seeked. You were terrible." She giggled at the memory. "I could hide for days." Her voice turned sad. "Then you went to Hades and I never saw you again." A tear glistened beautifully down her cheek.

Awww. She was guilting me out. I hated being guilt-tripped. I attributed it to my unbalanced personality problem. Worrying about Bethany, wanting to placate the batty nymph; my adolescent-goddess duality must have been messing with my hormones something awful.

I checked my watch. Still a half hour before class. I guessed I could squeeze in a few more minutes. "Why don't we—"

"Nysa." A very displeased Kai had silently arrived. Fabulous. Couldn't he walk up like a regular person? Dude was the poster child for abnormal and irritating behavior. He looked between Nysa and me.

I glowered at him in all his broody hotness and pulled my coat tighter around me, emphasizing my Michelin Man silhouette.

The only upside was that Nysa had gone pale. "K-Kyrillos," she stammered. Quickly, she pecked me on the cheek. "Gotta dash," she trilled in a shrill falsetto. She dove into the creek and vanished.

"I'm missing something here. Why is she so scared of you?"

Kai grinned. "I'm a very scary god."

"No. Seriously."

"Nysa used to drive you insane."

"That hasn't changed."

"First time she tried to follow you into Hades, you asked me to take care of it. I did. She never tried to visit you there again."

I was intrigued. "What did you do?"

"Nope. A god's gotta have his secrets. No mystery otherwise."

I laughed before remembering that I was mad at him. I think. Kai hadn't bothered to show himself to me since he'd dropped his bombshell on me and pronounced me his. For someone who protested so strongly against being considered human, he did an awfully good impression of a caveman.

He had me so confused, I didn't know what I felt toward him anymore. "So? Been busy?" I asked breezily.

"Yes. Dragon, remember?"

"She's back?"

"No. But I did find out a few things. Delphyne was the keeper of the Oracle. The site *and* the priestess. Guarded them. Once there was no more Oracle, she was out of a job. Evidently, she's been trying to find a suitable priestess ever since."

"Cassie." A thought occurred to me. "When my change set off Cassie's, she must have popped up on Keeper's radar. I wonder if that's what that truth exercise was all about? Her wanting to test if Cassie really was prophetic."

Kai didn't know what I was talking about so I explained what had happened in class that day. "Wouldn't be surprised," he said.

"So Delphyne's taken her to Greece?"

"Nope. No sign of her anywhere."

"Then she must be in Keeper's office behind window number one."

Holy crap. I had to go kill a dragon now. Guess I'd be missing class. "Be vewy vewy quiet. I'm going dwagon hunting." Because really, if you couldn't crack inappropriate jokes in the face of possible death, when could you?

Kai looked at me for a long minute before he sighed heavily and took my arm. "Come on."

"Thanks, but I'm good."

"You let a nymph guilt trip you. What are you going to do when the dragon turns her big brown eyes on you? Other than get roasted."

"Charming." I took in his stubborn expression, considered how much I felt like having this fight, and decided the answer was "not at all." "I'll let you come for guilt duty, but the dragon is mine."

"Go nuts."

Talk about making a girl feel special. Anymore sweet talk and I'd behead him myself.

I brightened. So long as there was a plan.

11
United we stand, deluded we fall
ια´

We ran into Anil on the way back inside. "The divine Miz S," Anil enthused. He had a partly open sports bag slung over one shoulder, inside of which I could see his wrestling gear.

After my encounter with Nysa the spectacular (and spectacularly insane), my ego was desperate for any compliment. I took off my jacket, like that was going to up my appearance factor. "We have to stop meeting like this," I joked.

"Getting to be a regular event, I hear," Kai said, flashing Anil a smile that showed a little too much tooth. He placed his hand on the small of my back.

It was possessive and ridiculous and blatantly "mine is bigger than yours" posturing. I won't lie. I thrilled. For about two seconds. Then I opened my mouth to tell him to quit it precisely as he started stroking his thumb over my sweatshirt in feather light touches.

I squirmed, highly distracted.

Anil threw me an odd look.

"Someone must have walked over my gra-ve?" I ended on a squealed question as Kai slipped his hand under my top to continue with skin to skin contact. I was positive I was blushing.

"Whatevs. Catch you at dinner." He frowned at Kai, who smiled blandly.

The stroking didn't stop. "You've made your point. He's gone."

Kai's fingers trailed down my back to the top of my pants. "Maybe the point wasn't for him."

I met his gaze, refusing to be cowed into submission. Massaged into submission. Whichever. "You going to help me slay a dragon or not?"

"If I do, does that make me your knight?"

"If only you could be labeled so easily."

Kai laughed. How come he only sounded that entertained when it was at me, not with me?

"Why do I get the feeling that nothing else amuses you as much as I do?"

Kai's only response was an enigmatic smile as he towed me along to the gym.

Theo and Hannah were waiting. Hannah handed me a King Size package of Reese's Peanut Butter Cups.

I unwrapped it. "You got peanut butter in my chocolate."

"You got chocolate in my peanut butter," she answered, taking one of the cups.

We giggled. I offered the third one to Theo, who declined, so I rewrapped the rest and shoved it in my pocket for later.

"I'll have one," Kai said.

"There's a corner store in town. Go nuts," I mimicked. Take that, suckah.

"All caught up with the nymph?" Theo asked.

"Any other old friends I should reacquaint myself with? A man-eating python, a giant with anger issues? We could have tea."

Theo snickered. "At least we got the box."

Kai held out his hand to see it and Theo tossed him the box. Kai turned it over, not looking enormously impressed.

"It expands when we open it," Theo informed him.

"No kidding."

I attempted to take it from Kai. He held it away from me. After a couple of useless jumps to retrieve it, I gave up and adopted a Western swagger. "All right, hoss, guess you're on box duty. But save the killin' fer me."

Kai scowled at Theo. "'Hoss?' Was there so little choice of available humans that you had to pick this one? Six billion and you get the one who should have been left on the hilltop to die?"

Hi-larious. As soon as the dragon was dead and Cassie safe (fine, and Bethany too), I was going to find a way to get Kai's ass expelled and out of my hair. "Let's do this."

"Try to remember everything about it," Hannah said.

"You're not coming?"

"'Course she's not," Theo said.

"I'm not a lethal weapon like you, Soph. I can't lock and load."

"I know, but we're a team. You, me, Theo." I pointed

at Kai. "Even Gilligan there. I just figured that you'd be by my side for this. I'll keep you safe."

Hannah hesitated.

I continued with my song and dance. "My whole life, I've listened to you go on about one deadly animal after another. You're obsessed with things but all you ever do is read about them." I took her hand. "You need to get out of your comfort zone. I mean, I know it's not easy, but you're sixteen. You can't spend your life secluded away. You gotta engage with the world in all its glory and danger. It's normal. Plus, we're talking dragon here."

"You just go for the emotional jugular, don't you?" Hannah muttered, pulling her hand away.

Despite knowing that this adventure would be dangerous, I wasn't callously disregarding Hannah's safety. I really believed that with the level of my powers, I could keep her safe. And I was sure she'd regret missing this opportunity for the rest of her life.

"Listen, if you believe that between Kai and me," I said, shooting him an "agree or else" look, "we can't protect you, then stay. But if anything I've said is true, then push yourself and come."

Hannah glanced uncertainly at Kai. "I'll watch your back," he assured her.

"We going or what?" Theo demanded. I think all of the sharing and the insights were making him nauseous.

"We're going,' Hannah announced. I squeezed her arm. She brightened. "I'd be an idiot to turn down the chance to see my phony school counselor in dragon form."

Kai looked puzzled. "How do you remember that?"

She grinned. "The miracle of flashcards. Helps you memorize anything. Even seemingly non-existent students and faculty. Give me one sec. I just need to race up and grab something."

I handed her my jacket and sweater to dump in our room. She returned momentarily wearing a couple of long scarves as belts. Hey, if she needed to accessorize to feel brave, I for one was not going to criticize her.

The door to Ms. Keeper's office opened easily. Either no one had been inside since Kai's and Theo's fight or Stan was getting lazy, because the debris remained. The warded up window still glowed blue.

Theo pulled out the dragon scale. "Watch and marvel." He said something in Greek under his breath, then swiped the scale in a complicated pattern against the invisible barrier. Theo released the scale and it fell through the windowpane freely. "We're good to go."

"Nice. How'd you do that?" I was definitely impressed.

"I figured the barrier was probably keyed to Delphyne's body. She had to be able to get through no problem. All I had to do at that point was make the ward believe that the scale was her entire self and let us through in one piece."

"Pretty fab," Hannah complimented.

Kai picked up a pencil and tossed it through the window frame. When it failed to set off any traps, he swung his leg over and hopped down.

Our unholy alliance was on its way. The blue glow provided some light, but Theo pulled out his chain, which immediately began to glow brightly enough to light our way properly. A corridor stretched before us, running about ten feet before it angled sharply left. We set off.

Every few feet, Theo would snap the chain forward in case any other traps were set. Since none of us were up for small talk, I took the opportunity to examine my surroundings.

Everything was rough. The floor was broken and uneven, like damaged cobblestones.

The walls were stone, although they were damp. Rivulets of water streamed down the sides and I was hit with the occasional drip on my forehead from the low ceiling.

From the way Hannah was manically swiveling her head around, I could tell she was committing every detail to memory for future examination.

"Happy you came?" I asked. She made a "shush" gesture at me and moved up ahead with Theo.

Kai laughed softly.

The corridor made a couple more sharp turns, then hit a dead end.

Theo turned to Kai. "Remind you of anything? Twisting paths, dead ends?"

Kai swore. "The labyrinth."

I twigged a past class lecture. "You mean like the Minotaur? We're going to run into a bull man?"

"I think the dragon is enough," Kai responded dryly.

There was too much hesitation and not enough saving going on. I pivoted and strode three whole steps back before I was restrained by Kai's hand on my shoulder. He spun me around.

"We're in a labyrinth. You do understand that word, right? Big maze designed to trap people. Usually with something very bad at the center."

"Don't talk down to me. I'm not an idiot. Nor am I helpless. I'll proceed with extreme caution, but lives are at stake here. So hurry up."

Kai sent a small blast into the stone walls. Just enough to scorch them, with minimal smoking. When I shot him a questioning glance, he replied, "We need to know which way we've been. To get out again." He continued to do this all the way through, differentiating between passageways which led nowhere and the useful ones.

We tried a different direction. Another dead end.

"Is this a common element of labyrinth design?"

"Yeah. It's a standard aspect of the 'you're screwed' school of architecture," Kai deadpanned.

I blinked in surprise, taken aback by Kai's sense of humor.

The corners of his mouth twitched up at my expression. "You're thinking there's hope for me, after all?"

"Let's not get crazy."

Theo snapped his chain down another path. It seemed safe. "Left?"

The rest of us shrugged in agreement. We'd find out soon enough if the path was useless.

We came to a large fissure in the wall and stopped to examine it. The air behind it was stale and stagnant.

"Structural damage?" Hannah asked, casting a worried glance up at the ceiling.

The thought of all this rock tumbling down on me was enough to give me a claustrophobia attack.

"Of sorts," Theo replied, darting a questioning glance at Kai, who nodded.

"You boys want to fill me in?" Anything to distract myself from the thought of being buried alive.

Kai traced the edge of the fissure. "I think Delphyne designed this labyrinth."

"Guardian of the Oracle and Maze Designer. She's a real Renaissance dragon." I would have preferred a double threat of singer/dancer, but apparently it wasn't my choice to make.

"You don't get it," Theo said. "'Designed' is the wrong word. More like created. The maze's existence is tied to her will."

"So?"

Kai pointed to the fissure. "It's coming undone."

Hannah frowned, puzzled. "Which means she's losing strength?" This could work in our favor.

"Which means she's losing her mind. My bet is she's come unhinged."

"Why now?" I asked.

"Who knows? Maybe the stress of the final push to her goal? Maybe just having kept a human form for too long?" Kai squared his shoulders and tried a new path. Theo, Hannah, and I followed grimly.

"Seems promising," Hannah commented, glancing

about the path. No sooner were the words out of her mouth than the floor dropped out beneath us.

"Ahh!" We were falling at impossible speeds into an inky nothingness. There was no way I wanted to find out what was at the bottom.

I shot a ribbon of light out with my left palm and wove it carefully around the others' wrists. With my right, I shot the light back up at the ceiling. It held like a giant Spidey web.

"Whatever you do," Kai warned, "don't look—"

Down. Too late. There we were, swinging in mid-air. Far far below us was what must have been an enormous fire, since I was able to see the bubbling flames so clearly.

I got woozy contemplating it. We began to sway. What was it with the Greeks and their unnatural love of all things fiery? Why couldn't they have an obsession with, say, death by chocolate?

"You ever going to learn not to look?" Theo chastised.

"Theo!" Hannah snapped. "That's not helping." She glanced at the ribbons nervously. "That's not gonna dustify us, is it?"

"Great, put that in her head," Theo muttered.

"N-no," I stammered, making sure to think only binding thoughts not killing thoughts.

My light ribbon dropped us down a few more feet.

"Easy, Goddess," Kai murmured.

"Soph, look at me," Hannah ordered.

I forced myself to make eye contact. We were swaying dangerously.

"I never told you this before, but I kissed Jason Fried in grade two."

"I liked him! I even put glue in his hair so he'd notice me."

Hannah shrugged. "Yeah. Sorry. He was cute."

"Some defense," I replied, aghast at the elementary school betrayal.

"Keep going, Hannah," Theo muttered.

I realized that I'd started pulling us up. Ah. "Nice distraction technique." I paused. "It was a technique, right?"

"You'll never know unless you get us back up top," she replied, smugly.

"Hurry it up, already," Kai said. "Hanging over an enormous open flame is not my idea of a good time."

"Then jump us up," I snapped.

"From dangling in mid-air? Not gonna happen."

The cauldron began to rumble. It was a familiar sound. Kind of like a geyser.

Yup. There it went. Boiling fire spat up toward us. I yanked us up and deposited Kai, Theo, Hannah, and myself on the other side of the hole in the floor, milliseconds ahead of the scalding liquid. It hit the ceiling and splattered around us, and only Kai's quick thought to send out a shield of black light protected us from a boatload of pain.

"Go!" he yelled. Hannah, Theo and I raced down the corridor and took the first turn we found.

"But, seriously. You were kidding, right?"

Hannah laughed.

Kai joined us.

"Neat trick," Theo commented.

"Thanks," Kai said.

"I meant Delphyne."

"She is one demented dragon," I panted.

"She's certainly showing a lot of creative, higher-thinking abilities for essentially being a giant lizard," Hannah observed.

A troublesome thought hit me. "If Delphyne is tied to this maze, what happens when we kill her?"

"It disappears," Theo said.

Kai looked at him darkly. "In the best case scenario. And when have you ever heard of a best case scenario in a labyrinth?"

"It's called positive thinking," Theo snapped.

Kai waved him off. "Positive thinking gets you positively dead. Be a realist and prepare for all contingencies."

"You have a Plan B?" I asked hopefully.

"Never fear."

The corridor lightened. "Must be getting close. To whatever it is." Theo kept his chain close.

Kai continued to mark the walls.

"You know what's still bugging me?" I asked. "What happened while we were in Hades that made Keeper want everyone to forget about Cassie, Bethany, and Mrs. Rivers?"

Kai thought about it. "Could be it was the first time she took her dragon form. She was stepping up her plan."

That made as much sense as anything else. I was about to say so when I realized I was all alone. And in the dark.

"Hannah? Theo? Kai?" They were nowhere to be found. Had she just plucked them out of thin air? What did she have in store for me?

"Sophie," a slightly slurred voice trilled. Ice tinkled in a glass.

I checked my watch and groaned. The light slanting through the window at the far end of Felicia's living room was not yet in full brightness.

Not even mid-afternoon and Felicia was drunk already. "Felicia, you've had enough."

Felicia stared at me with lidded eyes as she nursed her gin and tonic, then motioned for me to sit. She smoothed out her already perfectly coiffed blonde hair and flexed a Christian Louboutin pump in my direction.

I sunk into my favorite overstuffed chair. Out of habit, my toe wriggled its way into the chip in the fireplace tile beside me. It drove Felicia nuts when I did that.

Today was no different.

She snorted. "What am I going to do with you?"

"Get your money back?"

"If only I could. Get a decent pair of shoes for you. Never really wanted you, you know. Guess your real mom didn't, either."

You'd think after sixteen years of this, I'd be immune to it. And I was. Mostly. Didn't mean she wasn't a bitch, though. Some thought was tickling the back of my brain. Or was that something scratchy against my neck?

She held out her glass. "At least you make a good cocktail."

"Make your own damn drink, Felicia. I'm not your slave."

Felicia gave me a tipsy, mocking bow. "Forgive me, princess."

Princess? Yeah. I'd been stolen from royalty. Kind of?

"My real mom is a queen," I replied. "And when she finds how you've treated me, she'll be pissed. Royal wrath."

"Ooh, I'm terrified," Felicia taunted. She swung up into a sitting position and again thrust her drink at me. "Grow up, Sophie. And get me my drink or I'll take you away from your precious friends and stuff you in a military academy."

Grumbling, I swung my feet onto the ground and stood. I took a couple of steps toward her to grab the stupid glass but my feet got tangled in her precious Persian rug.

"Jesus! You're a walking suicide mission."

Ooh! I hated that phrase. And that stupid, arrogant, sanctimonious rat bastard Kai with his all-knowing condescension who kept saying it to me. I was a goddess, damn him.

Hang on. "I'm a goddess!"

Felicia looked startled. Then she laughed so hard she belched. I almost saw fire spew out, it was so potent.

"It's true!" I felt myself reverting to a childish status but I was so mad, it was all I could do to keep from stomping on the floor.

"Prove it," she mocked.

"Fine," I shot back. Except I had no idea how. I waved

my hands around. That seemed like a good place to start. Good place to end too, since it didn't do anything.

She rose and came toward me, rattling a small bottle. "Take some of my Chlorpromazine."

"I'm not insane. I don't need an anti-psychotic."

Felicia stopped in front of me and opened the bottle. "One little pill, Sophie. It'll make you feel better." She peered intently into my eyes.

My head hurt. Maybe she was right?

"Listen to mummy," she cooed.

Yes. My mom would make it all better. She loved me.

Felicia put a pill in the palm of my hand, then closed the bottle and handed it to me. "Take one now and as many as you like later." She closed my hand around the bottle. "You keep it. See how much mummy trusts you?"

I was the luckiest girl in the world. I put the bottle in my pocket, but it wouldn't fit. There was something else in there. I pulled out the chocolate candy and regarded it curiously.

"You got peanut butter in my chocolate," I murmured dreamily.

Felicia didn't answer. I frowned. That wasn't right. She was supposed to answer.

"You got peanut butter in my chocolate," I prompted again.

"Stop saying that," she snapped.

That wasn't the right answer. I said it again, quietly and mostly to myself. The answer pushed at my brain until I could hear Hannah saying "You got chocolate in my peanut butter!" I felt the hold on my mind relax. I'd remembered who and where I was. "Nice try, Delphyne," I taunted.

Felicia's face contorted in rage and transformed into the enormous visage of one very pissed off dragon. Smoke puffed out of her flared nostrils. Her face was more reptilian than I'd expected, and a slightly darker purple than the scale Hannah had found. Inhuman eyes stared at me with malicious intent.

I swallowed. I think I'd liked her better as Felicia.

Delphyne's body was behind me. She had coiled her long scaly neck around my body and Exorcist-twisted her head around to face me.

I squirmed and ducked to get out of her grasp, but she restrained me with a heavy claw on my shoulder. I tried not to look down at it, but I couldn't help myself. Yup. Four long, lethally sharp talons curved from the gnarled claw to bite into my shoulder. I could see the blood welling through the rips they had made in my shirt.

Maybe this would be the part where she told me to go back and she'd let me live?

Delphyne opened her mouth and sprayed flames. I tore out of her grasp just in time to avoid them. Problem was, I hadn't realized that her mouth wasn't necessarily the most dangerous part of her.

Her heavy, spiked tail lashed around to fling me like a tennis ball into the stone walls. I flew backward, hitting my head against the rock, and slid to the floor, lacking the useful bouncing properties of the aforementioned ball.

Blood trickled down my scalp, but as long as I was conscious, I had to fight her.

The ground vibrated with every step of her hulking body as she made her way closer. I was amazed she wasn't leaving cracks in the rock with each stride, as she had to weigh almost a ton. From nose tip to tail end, I guessed her to be close to ten feet long, and the top of her head stood about eight feet off the ground.

Better take my turn, and fast. I blasted her with a wave of powerful light. The knock to the melon and my awkward position meant I wasn't in perfect form and didn't kill her. Did leave a heck of a scorch mark across her side, though.

Delphyne hissed at me; her eyes wild. "You will not get the Oracle! She's mine!" With one more roar of flame, she fled down a corridor, into the shadows.

Any lingering doubts I may have still been harboring about the status of her sanity were gone with that look. Beastie was mad as a hatter.

And I was starting to feel a bit like Alice in Wonderland. It was all completely mad. Persephone, Delphyne, a war of the gods, betrayals, and murder. Best not to think big picture. Too overwhelming.

Immediate plan: find Theo, Hannah, and Kai, and charge to the rescue.

Unsure of where anybody was at this point, including myself, I picked a direction at random. I wasn't entirely rash. First, I collected a handful of broken cobblestones from the floor to toss in front of me as I went. No need to be surprised by any more nasty traps.

Well, nasty physical traps. Given that last little head game trick with Felicia, it appeared there was nothing I could do about the psychological minefields.

This corridor was dark. I released my light just enough to allow a faint ball to shine in each palm. I was like the deluxe edition of a human Swiss Army knife; handy in every situation.

I kept my eyes and ears peeled for any sign of my gang.

Now that the shock had worn off, I had to admit that my encounter with Felicia, even though it had been an illusion, had really shaken me up. It was as if years of Felicia's meanness had been distilled into two fun-filled minutes.

I shook my head. Of course. It *had*. Delphyne didn't have some intimate and interactive acquaintance with Felicia. Everything she'd thrown at me had come from my memories. Even the Chlorpromazine. It was all drawn from my real life and woven into this tapestry of lies.

My conscious self must have been attempting to break through the illusion. Maybe the fact that I'd managed meant that I was more capable than I gave myself credit for? Maybe I hadn't been useless, run-of-the-mill Sophie all these years; a girl who happened to luck into these powers?

What if my laying low was subconsciously part of some bigger cosmic plan? The very thing I'd needed to do—be a normal, unexceptional human—so that my powers would matter when I came into them?

I rounded a corner feeling a renewed sense of confidence.

If I'd been Einstein or Serena Williams, perhaps they wouldn't have had such an impact. Since I would have already been exceptional, maybe I wouldn't have wanted to give my life up to fight a battle that was my backstory and not my present.

Even Felicia made a twisted kind of sense. Would I be so willing to charge in and right the wrongs if I had to worry about a loving family? Worry about them not only getting harmed, but becoming horrified by me?

How would a good mom have felt seeing her little baby become a mutated freak of nature? She might never have recovered, and that would have devastated me.

Felicia wouldn't care. And I realized that was for the best. I was feeling good. I'd made some important realizations about myself; I hadn't set off any more traps.

In all ways, it appeared as if I was on the right path.

Then I hit it.

No. Not a dead end.

A dead body.

12
A little carnage is a dangerous thing
ιβ′

I screamed like the frightened little girl I'd just reverted to as reality smacked me in the face.

Pyrosim and Photokia were one thing. This was worse.

Mrs. Rivers was dead. She lay face down, but I knew it was her even as I wished upon every wish that it wasn't. I collected myself as best I could, which meant the screaming stopped but the shaking didn't. Then I knelt down.

My knee landed in a patch of something dark. Blood. It was blood. Another scream threatened to spew out of me like vomit. I swallowed it down and took several gulping breaths to calm myself.

Then I gingerly rolled her over.

Her neck had been slashed, leaving a red gash like a twisted parody of a smile. Tears welled in my eyes. Back out in the real world was her family, who were never going to get her back.

If the enchantment wore off, and they did remember her, they'd never get closure on her disappearance. I couldn't carry her with me, and doubted I'd be able to get her out. Which meant that this stupid, messed up illusion was her final resting place.

She didn't look scared. That was a blessing. In fact, she appeared furious. She'd been killed in mid-snarl, her fingers twisted into talons. The woman had obviously fought back.

Good for you, Mrs. R., I silently cheered. A flutter of gold fabric in her right hand caught my attention. Carefully, I pried it from her grasp. It was a piece from the shirt Cassie had been wearing the last day I saw her. She'd died protecting Cassie, if not Bethany, too.

"Mrs. Rivers ..." I faltered. "You were a great counselor and kind person. We all really liked you." Could I have sounded lamer? I cleared my throat. "I'm so sorry this happened to you. You should have grown old and gotten sick of us kids, not died for us." With my left hand, I closed her eyes out of respect. "Goodbye."

I stood there a moment, feeling useless.

I wasn't sure what else to do. I couldn't bury her.

But I could avenge her.

I set off.

Theo was right. Being raised human meant my alliance fell with them. Perhaps, if I'd still been Persephone, I wouldn't have cared about Cassie. Or maybe I would have understood Delphyne's position better. After all, she was a creature trying to fulfill her own duty; that of guardian of the Oracle. Would I have applauded and respected the extremes that Delphyne had gone to in order to accomplish what she'd been born to do?

I was so preoccupied with my thoughts that I almost tumbled into a huge hole, too large to jump.

No problem. I shot a vine at a boulder on the other

side in order to swing myself across. The boulder glowed so white hot, I could feel the heat suffusing into my ribbon of light.

I started to sweat as I attempted to pull my vine away. The heat flowing into my arm grew to near unbearable proportions. And it seemed that the vine had fused to the white heat of the rock. I had to disconnect from it somehow.

I felt myself getting dangerously overheated. I shot a vine from my other hand at the boulder, which intensified the heat, but allowed me to destroy the rock.

The heat disappeared, which was great, but now I had no way across the hole.

I rested a moment, wiping off the sweat the best I could. I glanced up at the ceiling. I could attempt to shoot my light up there and swing across but I wasn't willing to risk that it had been booby-trapped in the same way. Dangling-crispy-Sophie was not how I wanted-ed to bite it.

"Hello?" I called out. My voice sounded muffled. It was as if I'd stumbled into some kind of dead zone. It creeped me out.

I couldn't go forward because of the hole, so I took a step back. There was a grinding noise and the walls to either side of me pushed in slightly. That couldn't be good.

Maybe I could just run for it. I rapidly pivoted and tried to run back out the way I'd come. I bounced off an invisible shield and landed on my front, millimeters from the gaping maw.

The walls pushed in some more.

I really wished I could remember how I'd thought as Persephone. Maybe she'd have some brilliant solution to all this.

My few memories were all I knew of her. Like a movie slowly unfolding, but without any insightful voiceover to make me privy to Persephone's views on the world. If I couldn't get inside her head, then I only had my own experiences to guide me. Sixteen years of humanity to form my moral compass.

At that moment, lying on the edge of the precipice, I felt a clear distinction between right—saving Cassie and even Bethany—and wrong: what Delphyne had done to Mrs. R. But was that seeing the trees and not the forest? Was I getting hung up on the death of a single individual because I had a purely human emotional attachment to her? Would the traits that would win me the battle and defeat Delphyne ultimately cost me the war?

And did any of this even matter, I wondered, as the walls closed in even further, now mere inches from either side of me. One more thrust inward and I'd be smooshed.

A sudden longing for my real mother swamped me. Forget navigating boys and cliques, I needed her to safely guide me through the minefield of my continued existence. What if I couldn't find her? What if she didn't want to be found?

I had to acknowledge that possibility. Either through fear of some kind of reprisal for whatever had motivated a visit to Hades, foul play already done, or simply because my plans went against everything she'd taught me, maybe Demeter was going to stay away permanently.

In which case, I was on my own. And the only thing I could be certain of, was that right here, right now, I had save my own butt so I could finish off a dragon and rescue my classmates.

I couldn't use my goddess powers, so I had to survive this as my human self. With a touch to my pendant to center me and a deep breath, I did what humans had been doing throughout history.

I took a leap of faith.

More of a roll, really. I tumbled off the edge of the hole into the great unknown as the walls above me ground together.

Falling down the rabbit hole, or in this case, dragon hole, did nothing to stifle my anger at the entire situation. Luckily, I landed without too much incident or damage to my person, jumped to my feet, and strode off.

Hannah, Theo, and Kai almost collided with me as they rounded a corner. I didn't even pause, cold fury driving me.

Theo and Hannah hurriedly stepped back, out of my way. Kai merely raised an eyebrow at the naked thirst for revenge written on my face, then fell into silent step beside me.

"Want to talk about it?" he asked softly.

"Mrs. Rivers is dead." Behind me I heard Theo spit out a colorful curse. "Now Delphyne has to die."

Kai touched a fingertip to the back of my head. It

came away bloodied. His eyes darkened. "So she does," he agreed.

One more sharp turn left and we hit the center of the maze. My breath caught at the sight before me.

If I'd been asked what the center would look like, I would have guessed it was some kind of cavern, with various pathways branching off of it.

Instead, I found myself in the middle of a ravine. Hot sunshine blazed out of a cloudless, sea-blue sky. Unlike our ravine out back of Hope Park, this one was not trees and dirt, but rock formations. Enormous golden rock cliffs scaled away on either side. A lush, olive green foliage covered their upper third.

Below my feet was more rock, sculpted by eons of wind into small stone dunes.

"I never thought to see this again," Theo breathed. There was a catch in his voice.

"Where are we?" Hannah whispered in awe.

"The Ravine of Phaedriades," Theo said.

Uh, Dorothy, that didn't sound like we were in Kansas anymore. "We're in Greece?"

"Of a sorts," Kai explained. "We're in ancient Greece. Or a reasonable facsimile thereof."

Delphyne. "She willed all this into existence?" I asked in amazement.

"One determined dragon." Theo adjusted his hold on his chain for a better grasp. "She's this way." He led us off.

"How do you know?"

"Because that's where the Sibylline Rock was. Where the Oracle sat."

The stone ground was so uneven, that I had to watch my footing carefully. It would suck to get this far only to make easy snacking because I twisted my ankle.

Theo shot his arm out to stop us. He pressed us back behind a boulder and tilted his head down and to the right. "Look, but don't be seen," he whispered to me.

I peered over to where he'd indicated and exhaled in relief.

Cassie was alive.

Far below us lay a wide, flat section of rock, with a fissure grooved deep into it. Straddling the void was a stone slab, resembling a sacrificial table.

"Scootch" Hannah hissed. She jostled me over so she could see as well.

Cassie stood on the slab garbed in a white flowing robe, arms outstretched to the sky, head thrown back, chanting. We were still too far to hear what she said, but she radiated power.

"Cassandra reborn," Kai said.

A ring of unfamiliar trees formed a semi-circle behind her. Even though I'd never seen them before, I knew instantly what they were; could almost hear the song of their life calling sweetly to me, Persephone, their Goddess of Spring.

"Laurus Nobilis," I said, remembering. Even though they could reach almost sixty feet tall, these were maybe half that. Impressive nonetheless. Small, pale yellow-green flowers bloomed in pairs beside each leaf.

My hands itched to touch them. I sharply reminded myself there would be plenty of time for that. First, Cassie.

Delphyne lay at Cassie's feet, her heavy head resting on her front claws. Her eyes scanned this way and that, but as of yet, had not detected us up high. Every few seconds, her tail twitched violently. I shuddered, remembering my last encounter with that particular part of her anatomy. I had no desire to reacquaint myself with it.

Considering this was Hannah's first glimpse of a dragon, she was being weirdly quiet. I glanced over at her. She had her head in her hands.

"What's wrong?" I asked, trying not to sound scared.

"My head," she moaned. "It's killing me."

Theo stroked her back. "Take a deep breath, Saul. I think it's the disconnect of your memory loss and the visual proof of Cassie's existence. Your brain doesn't know how to handle it."

"What do we do?" I asked.

"Nothing." Hannah raised her eyes to mine. "I suck it up and we deal."

"We'll have to climb down. There's a path." Theo had assessed our options.

"Are you nuts?" I asked. "I'm not a goat. Kai can jump us down."

Kai shook his head. "Not without attracting a lot of attention, I can't. I'm not dad with his invisibility cap."

Theo gave me a gentle prod. "Get moving."

Fine. I resigned myself to taking the scenic route and hoped the path wasn't too narrow.

It wasn't. Because it wasn't a path. "You want me to scale the rock face?" I asked in disbelief as we moved into position.

"More like rappel," Theo encouraged. "It's like this. You do your brilliant light trick and lower us all down."

"I'm going to fight a dragon. Do I have to deal with heights, too?"

Theo looked at me sternly. "Get over it."

I wanted to tell Theo that I hated his stupid self.

Except how could I get mad at the guy who'd given up everything to keep me alive and save humanity?

I scowled and stomped off.

Theo followed me. "You're so pissed right now. But you feel guilty so you're keeping quiet."

Argh! He knew me too well.

He broke into a grin. "Your eye is twitching."

I slapped a hand over my eye, which was, in fact, twitching. "You done?"

Theo chuckled. "Magoo, it was my decision to save you and pay the price. You've got nothing to feel guilty about."

"Really?"

"Really." He shrugged. "Unless you screw up. Then I'm going to make you feel soooo bad."

"I hate you."

He smiled. "Feel better?"

I grinned back at him. "Yes."

We returned to Kai and Hannah.

I looked down and groaned. "I'm gonna throw up." It was too far.

Kai stifled a laugh at my discomfort.

I shot him a "not funny" glare. "You think it's so easy? You do it."

"I don't do ribbons. Kai smash with destructive beams."

Muttering what part of him I wanted to smash, I snaked out the light of my right hand to wrap around Theo and Kai, binding them close together in a very homoerotic Greek hug.

Man, were they annoyed, but I had to get my kicks where I could.

"I don't want to know what you have planned for me," Hannah muttered, massaging her temple.

"Baby," I flirted, "we're going to be closer than we've ever been."

With the light from my left hand, I bound Hannah to me. Now that we were all trussed up together, I wrapped the ends of both ribbons snugly around a large rock at the lip of the cliff.

"It's not a present, Martha Stewart," Kai growled. "Get on with it."

The four of us shuffled awkwardly to the edge. Hannah, Kai, and Theo because that's the only way they could walk given their bindings and me because, well, I was scared out of my tree.

"The first step is the hardest," Hannah said brightly.

"Then it's all downhill," Theo added.

"Couple of real weisenheimers you—" The rest of my sentence turned into a smothered shriek as Kai jerked hard to the side to unbalance me and cause me to tumble off the rock.

When my terror had abated to mere mind-numbing fear, I managed to stop our fall so we could sway in mid-air while I hyperventilated.

"Now would be a good time to close your eyes and not look," Theo said. "Just lower us down."

Slowly, I let out my light, jerking us down the rock face. It didn't matter that we careened into outcropping brambles and random foliage. Nothing was going to keep me from my plodding journey to reach the ground.

I almost kissed the rock once my feet landed safely on terra firma.

"Damn girl," Theo groused, rubbing his neck. "I've seen smoother plane crashes."

Kai touched a scratch mark on his arm that was bleeding from a branch. "Next time I'm risking the jump."

So, no thanks there. At least Hannah patted my arm supportively.

Now at the bottom of the ravine, the four of us crept along the rock wall until we could peer around it for a closer view of Cassie.

We were in hearing range now. I strained my ears to catch what Cassie was saying.

"*One to overthrow. One to face the dark. One to lose it all.*"

Just once, I'd like that girl to say something like "one to have a nice day," or to spew winning lottery numbers.

Separating us from her rock was a small body of water. I couldn't see it since that would involve breaking cover to edge toward the lip of the rocky ground I stood on and peer down, but I could hear it babbling below us.

A narrow, precarious rock bridge connected our rock formation to theirs.

"That thing looks like it'll crash into the creek if we even step foot on it," I said quietly.

"Not creek. Castalian Spring," Theo corrected.

"Whatever. We better cross it one at a time, and quickly."

"Not so fast, Speedy Gonzales," Hannah said. "Smell that?"

I sniffed the air and caught a whiff of a sweet smelling gas.

"The Oracle didn't just predict the future because she was psychic," she explained. "She was high." She nodded toward the spring. "Full of Ethylene. A narcotic."

"Cassie wasn't high when she gave me my truths in class."

"Yeah," Theo said, "but this is running predictions all day, all night. Girl needs a little pharmaceutical assistance."

Hannah looked toward the water, thoughtful. "Since the spring runs around that rock, the closer we get, the more we'll inhale. Couple of minutes and we'll be chanting, too. But not coherently."

"So we have two minutes," Kai said. "Plenty of time." He seemed impatient to get going.

He could wait another second. "Was Delphyne going to just keep Cassie here indefinitely?" Maybe having some insight into what she'd planned would give us an edge.

Theo nodded. "Til Cassie died. Yeah."

I shot Theo an exasperated look. "Then what? Rampage the world for some other unsuspecting descendent?"

"Why rampage when you can train the handmaiden," Kai said.

Kai's words didn't make any sense and I told him so.

"One Oracle, many lesser priestesses," he explained. "Conceivably, one could be trained to fulfill the duties."

"And she got her spare how? Mail order?" Oh. Of course. "Bethany." I spied her royal bitchiness just as her name came out of my mouth.

She had emerged from between the laurel trees, also garbed in a white flowing robe, with a black tattoo woven around her upper arm. She held a wriggling snake.

Years of hanging with Hannah, lover of all creatures deadly, enabled me to instantly recognize the scaly darling as a small Python.

"Seems Bethany's been reunited with a not-so-distant member of her family tree. Cold blooded, tiny brain, so many traits in common," I said.

The others leaned in to watch as Bethany, a smug expression on her face, picked up a wooden cup from the ground and held it to Cassie's lips for her to drink.

"Whoa," Theo exclaimed. "Bethany is gorgeous."

"And then some," Kai agreed.

"Hannah, punch them for me," I said, looking to her for support. "Hannah?"

She was racing toward the tiny bridge. I shot my light out to yank her back, before she was seen.

"Let go," she said, struggling. "I want to be with Bethany."

"Are you all insane?" I glanced back at Bethany. On closer inspection, she did seem to be glowing with hotness. And a compelling confidence as she turned and strode back toward the laurel trees.

Hmmm. No boys, no luxuries, apparently willingly waiting on someone hand and foot? "Stupid cow wasn't abducted. Delphyne bought her support with those amped up looks."

"Good trade," Kai said.

I smacked him, then shook my shoulders out and psyched myself up. "Count of three. Keep an eye out for Bethany when we fire."

"Don't hurt her," Hannah begged.

"I won't." On purpose. I couldn't be held responsible for accidents.

"Theo and Hannah, you get Cassie."

Hannah nodded and pulled the scarves from her belt loops. She handed one to Theo. "Tie her legs. I'll do her wrists. She may struggle when we carry her, but at least she can't flail out and smack us."

"Smart," I commented.

"You thought I was just accessorizing, didn't you?" she retorted.

Guilty as charged.

I took a deep breath. "One, two, three." The second we bolted forward, Delphyne left her position at Cassie's feet and took to the sky with a screech.

Heavy purple wings unfolded from her back. The exact shade of her body, they'd been so cleverly folded against

237

her that I hadn't noticed them until they unfurled. I was amazed something that huge could fly so easily.

No time to gape. Out of the corner of my eye, I saw Theo and Hannah bolt for Cassie so I immediately sent my ribbons toward Delphyne in order to dust her into oblivion. They slid right off her scales.

Not a problem. Instead, I blasted wave after wave of green light at the dragon from my eyes and palms. I could have just destroyed her with my full-body shock-wave but since that would have taken out my friends, too, I was limited to single blast combat.

The waves flew from my eyes and my palms, rippling outward like a sonic blast of slaughter. Delphyne was taking some hard hits. In her pain, she howled high notes I wouldn't have thought audible to the human ear.

But my barrage barely slowed her down. She barreled toward me, talons out, spewing fire, focused in her madness.

I narrowly ducked a swiping talon to my face. Why was this hulking creature so much harder to kill than the regular minions that kept after me? She must have been higher up on the Greek mythology food chain than those peons, and thus imbued with more power, because I wasn't even causing one teeny scale to turn white with age.

Lucky me.

I reached the narrow bridge. I could cross it, but Theo and Hannah didn't need my help tying Cassie up. She wasn't fighting them, merely continuing to chant.

Since Delphyne was more than willing to travel to

me, I convinced myself there was no need to traverse something I'd probably trip off of anyway.

I had no idea where Kai had disappeared to. I tried to look for him between blasting and dodging but couldn't get a sense of his location.

Suddenly, something slithered onto my neck. I screamed and swatted at myself, hard. Bethany's python fell to the ground. I dove away from a particularly nasty roar of fire by Delphyne, who was bent on round thirty-six in the "kill Sophie, extreme fighting championships." I blasted the damn snake to bits.

"Rosie!" My head was yanked back by my hair as Bethany wailed on me for killing her pet.

"You insane bitch! Let go." I want some applause at this point for not just killing her outright and putting me out of my misery. I was still trying to honor Hannah's stupid rules about protecting humans. Or Bethany.

"When are you going to learn you can't compete?" Bethany glared into my eyes and I realized that Delphyne was not the only insane creature on the block. "I am the human incarnation of Beauty in the universe and all are drawn to me."

Then she decked me with a pretty beautiful right cross. As I stumbled back from the punch, she grabbed me and dragged me toward the bridge.

"Hannah!" I shouted. "Can I break the damn rule now?"

I saw her look between Bethany and me and hesitate.

Screw that. Shooting a ribbon of light from my palm, I wrapped it around Bethany's ankle and yanked her upside down so that we were face-to-face in a weird parody of the Spiderman kissing scene. Her arm with the tattoo dangled limply by her ear. This close up, I could see there was a small figure of a dragon woven amongst the laurel leaves which ran around her forearm. I guessed the tattoo was how Delphyne had given Bethany her mojo. Maybe I could amputate her arm some day. That would be fun.

"Listen up, skankass," I said. Out of the corner of my eye, I saw Delphyne land and raise her tail for a slashing of vicious proportions.

I'd fallen back into that same eerily calm center I'd been in when fighting the Infernorators and Gold Crushers. Or maybe I was just giddy at having Bethany where I wanted her.

Anyway, as Delphyne's tail whipped toward me, I jumped it like a skipping rope, then snapped my Bethany whip out to conk Delphyne in the head.

Bethany yelped. Delphyne roared and rose up on her hind legs. Gulp. She was really tall. I blasted the rock at her feet, causing it to crumble and Delphyne to fall backward. Her fire arced, useless, toward the sky. That ought to buy me some time.

Bethany screamed.

"Shut it," I snarled, as I swung her back for the rest of our quality time.

"Or what?" She postured. "I'm gonna tell Principal Doucette and you're going to be so expelled."

I blasted Delphyne with my right hand, knocking the dragon even back further, almost to the lip of the rock.

"Quiet, wannabe. Beauty fades but awesome goddess powers rock forever." I shook the still upside-down-and-reddening Bethany to make my point.

She spewed out a bunch more meanness, invoking all sorts of colorful slurs on my person, personality, and descendants.

Okay. So done with her. I tossed her to the side where she fell in a crumpled heap and finally, blessedly, stayed silent.

Delphyne didn't like that, either, because she renewed her attacks on me. I gave her everything I had.

"Aim for the eyes!" Hannah reminded me.

Score one eye and two. Delphyne screeched in pain.

Her loss, my gain. New and improved blind Delphyne had a much tougher time sensing me. "Good tip!" I yelled back.

For a such a big mother (and even blind), she was pretty good at dodging my hits. Even so, she should have been down and out by this point.

Exhaustion overwhelmed me and I got clumsy. Delphyne caught the right side of my body with her flames. I hit the deck, a Kindergarten chant ringing in my mind. Stop, drop and roll.

One more weak blast shot out of me. Uh-oh. Was the chamber empty? Seemed so. I was out. I lay on my back, spent.

Kai landed hard on his feet beside me.

"First off, stop doing that," I mumbled, pain fogging my brain. "And B, where the hell have you … ?"

Words failed me as I stared at Kai's true form. He towered above me, eighteen feet tall.

My jaw fell open as I craned my neck up to catch him in his unbridled splendor. Before me, truly was a god. Power and arrogance emanated from him. And gorgeousness. Definitely gorgeousness.

Any lingering illusion I'd had about the jerk being human disappeared. This was the Kai of my memories.

Delphyne was charging straight for us in a roar of teeth, tail, and insanity.

Kai looked down at me with what I swore was tenderness. Before I could make sure, it had been replaced with pure savagery.

I saw him raise his hands for the final attack.

No way. "I told you. She's mine," I snapped, as I sucked up every bit of energy in me and fired it outward from my palms at Delphyne a single blinding detonation.

I felled her in mid-charge. Her body twisted up into a gross arthritic knobbiness as her scales turned white. She spasmed violently on the ground.

Yay. Dragon down. But so was I. There was no way I was getting to my feet on my own power. Hating to ask, I rolled my eyes and stuck out my hand.

Kai was instantly at my side. With one massive hand, he carefully helped me up. "You are so stubborn. Couldn't let me take her, could you?"

Determined to stand on my own, I tugged my hand free. My knees buckled. I dragged my sorry self over to a large rock and propped myself against it.

Once I'd positioned myself in a suitably "I'm just

lounging, not actually using the stone to keep myself upright" manner, I felt free to respond to Kai's accusations of stubbornness. A quality I may have been on a first name basis with, but still.

"We discussed this. You were on box duty." Wearily, I raised my head to look at him, then blushed furiously as I realized that I was staring up at his groin.

Kai laughed. "Interesting possibilities," he murmured, which came out more like a rumble that bounced off the cliff walls.

"Such a dog," Hannah said, since she'd have had to be deaf not to hear his last comment. She and Theo had arrived with Cassie, hands and legs tied up in the scarves, strung between them. Hannah had the head, Theo the feet. Thankfully, Cassie had stopped chanting.

"You okay?" I asked Hannah.

"Except for my head trying to self-destruct. You were very impressive. Nice to see you showing some initiative."

"Ha. Ha."

"Good move finding the chalice," Theo said to Kai.

I glanced between the two. "Huh?"

"Delphyne was getting some extra help strength-wise. She must have known you'd be coming for her. So she got a chalice of power. Once Kai destroyed it—"

We lurched sideways, fighting for balance as Delphyne, still down but not out, whacked her tail several times against the ground, triggering a small earthquake.

"Delphyne was more vulnerable," I finished, once the rocks had calmed. "So I could take her down."

"You shot the killing blow," Kai conceded. He looked

back at Delphyne thrashing on the ground. "Almost killing. Theo, we need the chain. She's fighting hard. It's the last vestiges of her amped-up power. We won't be able to cut off her head otherwise."

Theo hesitated, then placed Cassie's legs on the ground, so that only Hannah was holding her body.

He pulled the chain out and cautiously approached Delphyne. With a swift flick of the wrist, he snapped the chain around her legs, binding them to her tail as if it was a fifth leg.

Delphyne roared in fury but held still.

Kai pulled a blade from his belt. He offered it to me, but I shook my head, still catching my breath on my rock. An eighteen-foot god would have better luck with decapitation than I would. "I'm good. Go for it."

He studied her neck, trying, I guessed, to determine the best site for the kill. As he considered, he twirled the knife in a weird pattern between his fingers. Neat trick.

"Save the foreplay for some other time," Theo admonished. "Cut off her head and shove it in the box already."

Kai gave him a mocking bow. He raised his hand and in a slashing motion, brought the knife cleanly through Delphyne's neck.

Her high-pitched death wail ended abruptly, leaving a deafening silence as her head rolled toward my feet. I jumped out of the way.

Kai bent and wiped the blade clean on the ground before returning it to his belt.

Theo motioned to Kai. "Box."

Kai tossed it and Theo opened it using some kind of

pressure. The box unfolded itself to a size more capable of containing the head. Kai placed it inside and the box resealed itself.

A loud rumbling issued from deep within the cliffs. Boulder sized pieces began to fall. Now that Delphyne was dead, the maze was unravelling.

"Get Bethany," Hannah ordered.

We were definitely going to have to work on Hannah's attitude adjustment where Bethany was concerned. "How do we move the head?" I yelled in a panic. That box had to be really heavy.

"Kai will have to carry it," Theo said, ducking falling rocks as he and Hannah rebalanced Cassie. I looked over to Kai for confirmation, but couldn't see him. How did one misplace an enormous male?

"Kai?" I jumped out of the way as a nasty big rock crashed down beside me.

Theo turned around and swore with a fury I'd never heard before.

"What?" I asked helplessly.

"He's gone."

"He must be around here somewhere. Why would he leave us?"

Theo pointed at Delphyne, dead and headless on the ground, but no longer bound. "Because he wanted my chain."

I couldn't believe it, but it was true. Kai had left, taking the chain with him.

Hannah shifted Cassie's weight and fixed me with a grim look. "We've been played."

There was no time to get answers for the tons of questions rattling around in my brain. Delphyne's fun house was unravelling, and fast.

I yanked Bethany to her feet none-too-gently.

Then I looked at the massive cliffs that were rapidly collapsing. "How am I supposed to get hold of those things long enough to propel us back up? Our way out is on top." Panic laced my voice.

"We have to try," Theo urged. "Fast."

I tried to run and take Bethany with me, but she dug in her heels and fought me with all she had. Enough of her.

"You want to die here? Fine!" Exasperated, I let her go.

She immediately bolted back toward the narrow stone bridge. "Hey! Get back here."

"Follow her!" Theo roared over the now deafening noise of an avalanche of stone.

I hesitated for a millisecond and he shoved me. Dodging the deadly debris as best I could, and shooting what I hoped were preemptive blasts upward to break up the larger pieces, I took off running, not allowing myself to think what would happen if the bridge crumbled beneath me as we practically flew over it.

"Bethany has awesome survival skills," Theo yelled, "She wouldn't have gone this way if there wasn't a reason."

He and Hannah sprinted along, holding a once again chanting Cassie. Hopefully she'd remember some of what she was saying later, because I didn't exactly have pen and paper to write it down.

We'd cleared the stand of laurel trees by this point, only to find a cave opening in the rock face behind them.

We dashed inside. Bethany stopped by a rock at the back of the cave and murmured some words.

A portal glowed.

Of course. If I was a crazed not-so-mythical beast kidnapping and killing to further my obsession with fulfilling my duties, I'd have built a back door into my madhouse as well.

Without thinking, I shot a ribbon of light from my right hand to grab onto Theo, Hannah, and Cassie, and with my left, sent my light straight across the cave to grab Bethany's ankle as she stepped through.

Momentum pulled us forward, but not fast enough. The portal was rapidly closing and we were nowhere near close enough to get through it.

So I did the only thing I could. With a snap of my wrist, I sent everyone else flying through the portal. They made it through as the portal winked out, leaving me behind in the cave.

Which wouldn't have been so bad if the next thing that happened hadn't been that this entire reality with me in it, ceased to exist.

13
Like father, like son-of-a-bitch
ιγ′

Yeah, yeah. I didn't cease to exist. Artistic license and all that. Sheesh. Give a girl a break.

Delphyne's alternative "reality," however, did totally blink out of space and time. Luckily, that was a fraction of a second after I got out. When I finally had the chance to look back, I figured that the extreme amount of energy that Delphyne had put into the labyrinth in the first place, took a certain amount of time to break down. Lingering echoes of her will.

Here's how my escape played out. Right as the portal closed, the bottom dropped out of the cave and dumped me in the spring below.

Stinky water filled my eyes, nose, and mouth. I couldn't breath; I couldn't tell which way was up.

I was convinced I was going to die as I was buffeted every which way by torrents of H2O. No longer a gentle (albeit odiferous) body of water, the currents now swelled violently, threatening to drown all in one final act of reclamation.

Mr. Locke's favorite phrase from *Romeo and Juliet*

sprung to mind; "good night, good night/parting is such sweet sorrow."

What an absolute crock. Parting may have been sweet, but dying was messy, thrashing, choking misery. Also, my life didn't flash before my eyes. (How ironic would that have been to finally see my life, in all its Persephone entirety, right as I bit it?)

Instead, a pale hand waved in front of my face. *Death wears blue nail polish?* I thought. Then died.

Fine. Fainted. Next time you're drowning and black out, tell me you didn't think you were dead.

I came to blinking at a viciously bright white light. Not sure if I was in Heaven, Olympus, or an entirely different afterlife, I tried to be clever about getting my bearings.

I always liked stories in which people played dead to fool their captors. Granted, I thought I was dead, but I figured the principal held true for a subtle sussing out.

"Finally," a female groused. "Like I've been sitting here for a gazillion and two hours."

That voice. What could I have possibly done to deserve to spend eternity with Nysa? I opened my eyes.

There she was, half out of the water, filing her nails. "You gonna get up already, lazy bones?"

I pushed myself up onto my elbows in surprise. I was in the creek back at Hope Park. Aware that I was laying in less than two feet of water, I tried to reconcile how Nysa could be half emerged from the creek. While she was definitely standing, unless she'd suddenly gotten a ridiculously short pair of legs, I had no clue where the rest of her was. "I'm not dead?"

Nysa laughed. A beautiful sound reminiscent of perfectly crafted wind chimes. Hell, she could have sounded like a donkey braying and I would have found it lovely at this point. "Big silly. I don't hang with dead guys. Icky!"

I heaved myself out of the water. "You saved me. Thank you." My appreciation was enthusiastic.

She shrugged and bit off a hangnail. All class, that girl.

"How did you know where I was?"

"Prometheus. He sent out a super signal."

"But I wasn't even in this world."

"No matter," she replied. "If it has water, I can get to it."

"I could kiss you."

She blushed, gazed down as if embarrassed, waved a hand at me, then with a flip, dove into the water and disappeared.

Ohmigod. Nysa had a crush on me. Persephone. That's why she was always around. She didn't want to be me, she wanted to *do* me.

A weird thought but flattering nonetheless. I had a moment of feeling bad that I didn't reciprocate. Liking someone who didn't like you, sucked.

Take me, for instance, and the stupid male who had betrayed me and left me to die. I was still harshly crushing on him. How pathetic was that?

'Course I quickly realized that spending five seconds

in a relationship with Nysa would drive me to nymphicide, so it was probably for the best.

I wanted answers, but first I wanted to find my friends. And get out of these wet clothes. Was there even anything clean for me to change into? This goddess trip had been brutal on my wardrobe and it's not like I'd had a chance to do laundry in the past couple of weeks since my life had turned upside down.

Ten minutes later, I was pushing through the crowded hallways en route to my room. I had no idea what time it was. Given that I'd gone into Delphyne's maze this morning and the number of students milling about now, it could have been lunch or after school. I'd have to check.

I received more than one odd look at my soaking wet, filthy, and scorched self. Sadly, mass gratitude was not part of the package. Only a cemented weirdo status.

It wouldn't bode well if I'd missed yet another day of class. Not like I could give Principal Doucette a note reading "*Please excuse Sophie. She was battling dragons in order to save your students. Signed, her mother.*"

To access the stairwell up to the girls' dorm, I had to pass by the counselor's office. Or the faker formerly known as Ms. Keeper. I paused as I reached her door. I had to look inside and see if anything had changed as a result of us killing her.

I think I was still hoping that maybe everything had reset itself with Delphyne's death. That I'd open the door and find Mrs. Rivers, smiling as she attempted to locate a specific piece of paper among all her general clutter.

I brushed the dampness from my eyes and turned the knob. As I stepped into the room, I was tackled in a huge hug from behind.

"Don't ever do that again, you big stupid!"

I disentangled myself from Hannah and spun to face her. "Okay. That's nothing like 'thanks for getting me through the portal Oh Great and Glorious One.'"

"I thought you were dead."

"Me too," I grimaced, hating what she must have felt.

"Are you okay? Your head?"

She grinned. "Hamata pumped me full of migraine pills. Bliss."

"How long were we dealing with Delphyne? It must have been hours."

"About five minutes."

Curious and curiouser. I glanced over at the portal which looked like a normal window again. "Why is the window back to its regular self?"

"No clue. What happened after we got separated?"

How to answer that question? "I'll fill you in while I change."

Finally, I was dry and Hannah and I had reviewed everything that had just happened. She explained how the moment Delphyne died, she could remember everyone clearly. Which was great except it also meant she understood what she'd lost with Mrs. Rivers. We both shed more than a few tears over her.

Hannah was unsurprised at Kai's behavior. "What did you expect?" she chastised. "He's a god."

"You sound like you're excusing him," I protested.

"I'm not. But I think we all assumed he would act like a human. That was our fault. It's like expecting a tiger to act like a house cat just because there's a furry resemblance. The tiger will tear your throat out when you pet it and it's your fault for thinking otherwise."

Intellectually, it made a certain amount of sense. Emotionally, I wanted a rally cry to cut off his balls. I had to console myself with putting on grey leggings and a cute tunic and stuffing my feet into extremely warm, comfy suede boots. Fortified, I took a last glimpse in the mirror.

"Ready?" Hannah wanted to go find Theo and Cassie.

I nodded, then grabbed her in a huge hug.

"What's that for?"

I released her. "If it hadn't been for our friendship and all our silly rituals, I would never have broken Delphyne's hold on my mind."

"Yeah, well. I'd hate to have to break in another best friend. Took me years to train you properly."

I grinned at her. She grinned back. "Okay. Moment over," I said. "Move your butt, Swedeling, and let's find the Rock."

That took a while. We searched his room, Cassie's room, the sick bay, the front office and the library. We couldn't figure out where they might have gone.

"Cafeteria?" Hannah suggested.

"The place of food? Why yes, we should look for him there."

Theo and Cassie were seated over hot drinks and a plate of freshly baked muffins.

"Muffin!" I squealed, realizing how ravenous I was.

Cassie looked up, pale but happy at my approach. She pushed her chair back as if to get up, but I motioned for her to stay where she was. "Sit. You need to get your energy back."

She thanked me profusely.

"Do you know exactly what happened?" Part of me was curious to find out if she remembered my real identity.

"Some of it. Some Theo told me."

Cassie filled us in. My suspicions about the truth exercise were correct. Ms. Keeper had only assigned it to see what Cassie came up with. It turned out that I had popped up on Delphyne's radar and brought attention to this place, and Cassie with it.

I apologized, but Cassie waved me off saying it wasn't my fault. She explained that when she said those "truths" about me, Ms. Keeper had started to press her on other things. When Cassie had gotten freaked out by her intensity, Ms. Keeper drugged her.

After that, Cassie had been kept in a zoned out state. Everything was dreamy until she found herself gagging on a potion Theo made her drink that cleared her mind.

"Do you remember all the truths you'd said to me? The prophecy?"

Cassie nodded. "I do."

I leaned forward eagerly. "What did it all mean? Am I really an 'instrument of destruction?' And the other stuff in the ravine? Something about the dark and overthrowing?"

She must have heard something of the bleakness I felt in my voice, because she squeezed my hand in a reassuring manner. "Not everything is literal. These things I see, that I say, they're fragments of truth."

"Not the whole picture?"

"More like maybe the whole picture but you have to know how to interpret it."

"You need the key," Hannah said.

We turned and looked at her. "Cassie," she continued, "when you were zonked on Chlorpromazine, you said something about a key."

"OneaboveonebelowakeyawakeitisnomoreITISNO-MORE," I chanted. They looked at me, bemused. "It stuck in my brain."

"Anyway," Hannah shook her head at me, "could the key be a metaphorical key, rather than Sophie being a literal key to something?"

"Sure."

Not much of an answer. I'd hoped maybe Cassie could clear up a few things, not make them more convoluted.

"Sorry, Soph. Guess I don't fully get how to use my own power."

"Can't fault you for that. I'm in the same boat." Not to mention all the questions I couldn't answer. Like why had I been in Tartarus? Why had Demeter wanted to come to Hades that fateful night? What, if anything did my pendant do? What did all of Cassie's predictions mean? Who had wanted me dead? And how could I get my memories back in order to figure out the way to save humanity?

I was broken out of my reverie by Theo asking Cassie a question.

"What about the blood that you saw?"

"That one was clear. Wish it hadn't been. It was Mrs. Rivers." Cassie turned haunted eyes to us. "She died in a pool of blood, didn't she?"

"Yes," Hannah replied.

"I thought as much." She gazed down and plucked at her sleeve. "I never saw her. Not physically. But I did 'see' her death. It was because of me."

"No," I insisted. "It was because of Delphyne. You were both victims."

"Is Delphyne going to stay dead?" Cassie asked anxiously. "Since you left the box back there and all?"

"Even if someone did find the box and manage to open it without invoking its self-destruction properties, there's no way to reattach her head and bring her back to life. She's gone." Theo sounded certain. I decided to believe him and have one less thing to worry about.

"Besides, the entire dimension is gone." I caught them up on what had happened. Then I hugged Theo. "Thank you. For everything, but most especially Nysa. You both saved me."

Theo shrugged. "Just sent out the bat signal, is all."

Dragon dead? Check. Cassie rescued? Check. "What are we going to do about Bethany?"

"She wasn't a victim," Theo said.

"Bethany was just herself," Cassie agreed. Even through the fog of the drugs and the water from the springs, Cassie had thought Bethany's behavior reprehensible. "She was getting off on it."

Speaking of Bethany … "Hannah, I know you think Bethany is this fabulous—"

"I'm over it."

"Really? Is she back to normal levels of toxicity?"

"Not exactly," Hannah replied. "Whatever Delphyne did to her in terms of her looks has stuck."

"She's supermodel amazing," Theo clarified.

"Yes. Thank you," I snapped.

"And she still gives off this charm. Or something that makes people look twice, want to get to know her. But it's not like it was back at the ravine. I don't feel like I'll die if she won't be my friend," Hannah said.

"That's good." I was relieved. I had no idea what I would have done if Hannah had crossed to the dark side.

"Yes and no," Theo said. "The fact that the enhancements that Delphyne gave Bethany remained means that the line between mortals and gods is blurring. We don't want humanity to be aware of us. Hannah excepted. And we definitely don't want humanity messing around with gifts they don't know how to control."

"So we keep a closer eye on Bethany."

"If Bethany knows who you really are," Hannah fretted, "it could be a problem."

"Eh. I'll kill her if she talks."

"Subdue her," Hannah corrected. "Still ixnay on the killing of humans."

Cassie paled. I patted her hand reassuringly. "Don't

worry, Cassie. You and I are freak sisters. We have to stick together."

She nodded her head thoughtfully. "We do."

"If you really want someone to kill, my vote is Kyrillos." Apparently, Theo was still very very angry over the loss of his chain.

"Explain something to me," I said to him. "I get that it's wrong to steal and he absolutely should not have taken what was yours. But you acted as if it was a big manipulation."

For a second Theo looked as if he wanted to rip me a new one for even asking the question, then he sighed. "I keep forgetting. You really don't remember. It's like this—"

"That's my cue to go," Cassie said, rising. "I want to put this all behind me, not learn more."

"Don't think you can," Theo said gently. "It's not going to turn off."

She shrugged. "A well deserved rest then. I'm going upstairs to see if my roommate Jessica remembers me again. My life is going to take a bit of straightening out." With a final thank you, she left.

"Back to the chain—" Theo began.

"It was personal to you. Because of what Zeus did with it," Hannah offered.

"Yes, but—"

"And the fact that you're still here, using it instead of it using you, is proof that you won that battle," I finished proudly.

"Whose story is this?" he asked.

We gave him meek looks begging forgiveness. It worked not at all, but he did explain what he meant.

"It's like this. Everything you said may be true, but this isn't about me. It's about what that asshole is using my chain for. You know Hades was poisoned, right?"

We nodded.

"He's vulnerable right now. More so than ever before. Now, think about it. If you were Kai and you hated your dad and you came across a magic chain that could bind him up, allowing you to say, stuff him in a magically enclosed cave, what would you do?"

"Steal it," Hannah groaned.

"Right," Theo continued. "And his accomplice would appear to be ... ?"

"Ah," Hannah replied.

Theo gave a tight smile.

Despite the fairly conclusive evidence, I really didn't want it to be true. Was everything Kai told me a lie? "But why stick around? Why not just steal the chain beforehand?"

"He couldn't take it from me. The chain and I are, pardon the pun, bound to each other. My willingly turning it over to the dragon changed that."

"And of course, Kai would know." Hannah shot me a sympathetic look. "Sorry, honey, but it looks like he really did betray you."

"He left me to die." I couldn't get my head around that. "I mean, even if I did sort of understand why he took the chain, he still needs me for his grand plan."

"But he doesn't," Theo pointed out gently. "Kai gets

rid of Hades, he's in charge. He doesn't want world domination. Earth doesn't matter. It's like I told you, he was raised to care about the Underworld. And once he rules it, with all its minions, he'll either take on Zeus himself or just be happy with what he's got."

"He never cared much about Zeus," I murmured. "That was me." I stood up jerkily. "I'vegottago," I mumbled, fleeing in a rush.

Drama queening, I know. But be fair. Kai and Persephone had had this grand romance. They (we?) defied everything to be together; I'm not talking feuding families, but all-out war. For whatever reason, I still felt remnants of Persephone's feelings for him, coupled with my own. Whatever those were.

And if that didn't convince you, then give me a break. I was sixteen and the dude had done me wrong. Big time.

All I wanted at that moment was to bury myself under the covers and eat chocolate until I passed out.

An arm slammed me into the wall. "Oops." Bethany stood there, oozing malice.

Despite the fact that both students and teachers were in the hallway, no one noticed what she'd done. Or they didn't care. Maybe they were so used to her bullying me that it failed to register.

So while no one was coming to my aid, they'd sure notice if I eviscerated her skinny ass. I was going to start wearing a T-shirt that read "highly unfair."

Bethany leaned in toward me. "I know your little secret, Persephone."

Great. That answered that question. "Like you

don't have any. I wasn't the one who went along with Delphyne's plan to keep Cassie hostage. Not to mention, she killed Mrs. Rivers. Or did that not matter so long as you got what you wanted?"

Shockingly, Bethany showed a moment of remorse at the news about Mrs. Rivers. "I didn't know about that," she said. "And I didn't go willingly. I didn't know what had happened." Her gaze turned flinty. "But am I sorry for what I got? Not. At. All. I'm going to make your life a living hell."

"Did you not see what I was capable of?"

Bethany smiled coyly at a group of guys who practically ran into the wall in their desire to ogle her. "Yeah, but we're on my turf now."

"Because I don't go here?"

A group of girls ranging from much younger than us to a couple of seniors, sidled over. One shyly waved at Bethany as the rest hung around waiting for her to notice them.

She held her finger up imperiously in a "one minute" gesture. "All these students? They love me. And they'll do anything I want them to. Every single day. What are you going to do? Kill them all?"

She leaned in close. "Popular trumps everything. Even goddess. And I'm eternally popular now." Her expression hardened. "Don't think I've forgotten your lame attempts to get my boyfriend," she tossed out. "Hands off."

If she found him, she could keep him. They deserved

each other. His betrayal knifed through me again, the pain fresh.

It fueled my supreme pissed-offness.

I smiled at her with a menacing glitter. "You're forgetting one thing. I don't have to kill everyone. I don't even have to kill you." Calmly, I moved a lock of her hair out of her face.

"Mess with me and I'll scar your face so badly you'll be begging hobos for affection." I shot my gaze down to her tattooed arm. "Especially if I also rip your magicked up arm from its socket and blast it into dust. No charm, no looks."

I flicked the tip of her nose. "Nothing."

With that, I spun on my heel and walked off.

"Ms. Bloom."

Jeez, was I never going to get upstairs to my self-pity party? I braced myself, plastered a smile on my face, and turned to face Principal Doucette. "Yes?"

"Your mother is here. I saw her outside as I drove up."

For a second, I thought he meant Demeter. "What?"

"Felicia. She's out front."

This could not be happening. I'd battled a dragon, saved lives, and been royally backstabbed. Hadn't I suffered enough?

I guess those thoughts showed because Doucette arched an eyebrow. "Manners, Sophie."

"Yes, Principal Doucette," I sighed. I backtracked to the front door, located in the foyer beside the offices.

It wasn't a particularly grand foyer or anything. Red and white tiles were supposed to convey a cheerful first impression. There was a large board cluttered with announcements and posters and a couple of armchairs. I longed to just sink into one of them and rest.

Instead, I pushed my way out the heavy wood door. Something red fluttered in the wind, down at the end of the drive. Felicia. Standing there in her favorite red dress, having a smoke. Way to role model, mom.

I started down the drive toward her, wrapping my arms around myself for warmth. I was dressed for "cute," not weather. What could have brought her here? Unless she'd decided that I *was* on drugs when I'd phoned her the day after my memories awakened and had come to drag my butt into some kind of twelve step program.

Trust Felicia to take a few weeks before doing anything about her daughter's addiction, if that was the case.

Even though I headed for Felicia, it took me a while to reach her because she was all the way down by the main road from town, which bisected the school. Not bothering to look for me at all. Typical behavior from her. My bet was she was indulging in a bout of passive-aggressiveness, making me hike out to her as a petty way of voicing her displeasure for having to deal with me at all.

Finally, I reached her. She blew a plume of smoke in my direction, which I not-so-subtly waved away.

"Yes?" I asked, testily.

"What? No hug?"

Gritting my teeth, I stepped into her embrace. "Not so tight," I said. Even if she was mad, she didn't need to crush me.

"All the better to take you with, my dear."

I stiffened. The voice that had hissed in my ear had not been Felicia's. I shot up into the sky, tight in the arms of a disguised Gold Crusher.

Panic filled my chest. I was so tired and mad that I'd failed to pay attention to the line demarcating school property and, therefore, Theo's wards.

Okay, the fall might kill me, but letting him take me anywhere would be the more painful option. I focused my light at the guy but was blasted with electricity before I could do harm.

"I don't think so," he snarled.

The pain and crazy body spasming distracted me for the rest of the journey.

The Photokia landed hard on the ground and dropped me roughly at his feet.

I was in an enormous white and gold hallway. Sunshine kissed my skin at the perfect temperature and the sky outside was royal blue.

I'd been here before. I knew this place. I was back in Olympus.

And I was not alone.

I looked up until I found myself staring into the cold eyes of Zeus. Weakly, I pushed onto my feet, not that five-foot-five was any kind of advantage when faced with a twenty-foot god, but we do what we can in these situations.

He eyed me up and down. "Hello, daughter," he rumbled. "You're shorter than I remember."

End Of Book One

Acknowledgments

The first barrel of gratitude goes to my friend Sarah, without whom this novel would not exist. Thank you so much for all our Persephone talks and for your encouragement to run with the idea.

Huge love, as always, for my story editors. In this case, the lovely and talented Elissa, Sam, Frances, Corey, Deb, and Lynn. All of you helped to make this the book it is today. And no, I don't mean that in a threatening way. (Necessarily ... heh heh ...)

Also many thanks to all of my family, friends, and total strangers who were so incredibly supportive with the launch of my first book *Sam Cruz's Infallible Guide to Getting Girls*. None of you told me to keep my day job. Plus you laughed in all the spots that were actually supposed to be funny. *With* me not *at* me. Big hugs to you all for that.

Finally, though, my deepest thanks and the dedication of this book goes to my beloved daughter. Deciding that enough was enough, she put her foot down and insisted that if her mom was going to ignore her (I mean fall under the creative spirit), then it better be for a book that she was allowed to read. So thank you, my little ~~dictator~~ darling, for not only your request, but all your millions of suggestions which kept me "on track." Seriously though, you are my joy, my delight, and I'm thrilled to have written this for you.

THE FUN CONTINUES IN:

MY DATE FROM HELL

Sophie Bloom's junior year has been a bit of a train wreck. After the world's greatest kiss re-awakened Sophie's true identity as Persephone (Goddess of Spring and Savior of Humanity), she fought her dragon-lady guidance counselor to the death, navigated mean girl Bethany's bitchy troublemaking, and dealt with the betrayal of her backstabbing ex Kai (sexy Prince of Darkness). Now you'd think a girl could catch a break.

Yeah, right.

After everything that's happened, Sophie still has no clue how to fulfill her destiny. If only she could somehow retrieve her memories of being Persephone! So when Aphrodite strikes a deal that can unlock Sophie's pre-mortal past, what choice does the teen goddess have but to accept?

The mission: stop media mogul Hermes from turning Bethany into a global mega-celebrity. The catch? Aphrodite partners Sophie and her rat of an ex, Kai, to work together … and treat this suicide mission as a date.

Add to that the fact that BFF Theo's love life and other BFF Hannah's actual life are in Sophie's hands, and suddenly being a teenager—even a godlike one—seems a bit like … well, Hell. Whatever happened to dinner and a movie?

The romantic comedy/Greek mythology fireworks continue to fly in *My Date From Hell*.

Breaking up is easy; dating is deadly.

About the Author

Tellulah Darling
noun

1) YA novelist
2) Alter ego of a professional screenwriter/instructor
3) Sassy minx

Geeks out over: cool tech.
Squees for: great storytelling.
Delights in: fabulous conversation.

Writes about: where love meets comedy, flavored with pop culture. Awkwardness ensues.

Check out her other books, drop her an email, or help her procrastinate in some other amazingly time consuming way at: www.tellulahdarling.com.

CPSIA information can be obtained
at www.ICGtesting.com
Printed in the USA
LVOW08s1634260417
532272LV00002B/397/P